The One

The One Minute Dream

Colin Pearce

An Armada Original

877611

To Dr Charles Garlick, who did his best to teach me English at school, and a lot more besides; and to my family and friends who have fondly celebrated this small book with me; and to Jenni, who did the hard work.

First published in the U.K. in 1990 in Armada

Armada is an imprint of the
Children's Division, part of
the Collins Publishing Group,
8 Grafton Street, London W1X 3LA

Copyright © 1990 by Colin Pearce

Printed and bound in Great Britain by
William Collins Sons & Co. Ltd, Glasgow

One

Rosie had a dream; a burning ambition that never left her mind. She was determined to skate the entire length of the Esplanade in one minute, and she was determined to be the first to do it.

She had taken great trouble to work out the length of the Esplanade. To do so she first marked one metre on the ground with a ruler, then she practised making strides over the marks. They had to be long strides because, although she was twelve, she was not tall, and ordinary paces would have been too short.

When she was familiar with the exact size of a one metre step she paced out the entire Esplanade. From the flagpole outside the yacht club at the eastern end, to the railings at the western end, the Esplanade was 491 paces, plus an extra 38 centimetres that she measured with her ruler.

She had skated the length of it, red-faced, gasping and delighted, in 1 minute 20 seconds. That was her record, and she yearned to reduce it further still.

As time passed her dream became more desperate. She was growing, which was good because her long legs grew longer and her slim body grew stronger; but at the same time her skates grew older. The fabric of the boots was frayed and split and the day was drawing near when they would fall apart. Either that, or they would no longer fit her.

They pinched already. If she wore them too long she

suffered from cramp in the bottom of her feet and painful red sores on the joints of her toes.

She was saving for a new pair. She cut the lawn for a neighbour once a week through the summer (but this was spring) and her mother gave her a little pocket money every week. There was no dad to turn to. She had never known her father. He died when she was a baby. Her grandparents were all dead, too. Her mother worked in a supermarket, sitting all day at the till, agile fingers flicking over buttons while the cash register whirred and chimed and gurgled its sums. She worked Saturdays, too, but still there was never much money.

So new boots had to wait. She needed £30, and she had £15. If a chance came to earn more she grabbed it gratefully, eager to raise the rest before she could no longer struggle into the old boots, or they collapsed completely, or the price of the new ones increased. And there was another reason for her desperation: Bernard.

Bernard planned to beat her in her dream. He wanted to be first to skate the Esplanade in one minute. And Rosie punched her knuckles into the palm of her hand in impotent fury when she remembered it was her own tongue that had turned Bernard into a threat; in some ways even, into an enemy.

Rosie talked roller-skating in class, at break times and on the way home in the evenings. She talked about it to anyone and everyone – including Bernard.

Her freckled face lit up and a grin spread as she described the thrill of hurtling down the Esplanade, skirting pedestrians in a blur of speed, and spinning to an expert stop centimetres from the railings at the far end of the 491.38 metre dash. With wild and wide-eyed excitement she talked of her dream, her one-minute dream; and Bernard took it all in.

He was not like Rosie in any way. Rosie was slightly built, Bernard was tall and heavy. Rosie was a tightly-packed tin of something excitable that would explode like a Roman candle if ever the fuse was lit; Bernard was dignified and indomitable, like an ocean liner nosing its way through a fleet of little boats. Rosie's clothes were made by her mother from other clothes and had the faded look of hand-me-downs; Bernard wore smart, crisp clothes from expensive shops.

Rosie could keep no secrets. Everyone knew exactly how much money she had saved for her new boots; and when she trimmed another second off her best time the whole world knew it.

Bernard smiled secretly, made his plans and told no-one.

It was well known that Rosie was a good skater. No-one guessed Bernard's ability until he announced one morning at the school gates, 'I skated down the Esplanade yesterday – in one minute fifteen seconds.'

One or two nervous laughs died quickly. Was he joking? Eyes turned cautiously to Rosie. She was talking on the edge of the group and it took a few seconds for Bernard's words to invade her attention.

Her mouth froze open in mid-word. Before she could snap it shut it had given away her horror. The corners of her eyes crinkled as she narrowed them.

'Liar!' she spat.

'Dad timed me with a stopwatch.'

'I bet!'

'I'll show you if you like – tonight.'

'With everyone watching?' goaded Rosie. 'You wouldn't turn up.'

'I'll have to go home for my boots. I'll be there about half past four.'

7

Rosie watched his back as it cruised a path through the crowded playground. The others watched Rosie. She became aware of them and forced a laugh that everyone copied; but everyone knew, too, that Rosie's laugh sounded just a little bit nervous.

That evening Rosie and Bernard met on the Esplanade, and half the school met with them. Word had spread. They lined up along the low wall that separated the Esplanade from the road in front of the smart houses and the hotels.

Rosie was hypnotized by Bernard's boots. They were proper speed-skating boots: red and black leather with alloy skate frames and bearings that whispered over the ground. Rosie knew they cost twice as much, more, than the ones she was saving for. She reflected bitterly how many times, nose pressed to glass, she had admired them in the local sports shop window, next to the ones she was saving for.

Bernard warmed up for the race (for, although it had never been said, everyone knew this was not to be merely a demonstration by Bernard, but a race between him and Rosie). And he had brought his father's stopwatch as he had said he would. Rosie, who relied on counting the seconds to herself as she flew along the Esplanade, was furious and jealous and full of loathing. Maybe he had done it, just as he claimed. A nagging doubt rubbed at Rosie's mind.

Bernard gave the stopwatch to a friend; rules were agreed. They would start at the flagpole. One of the crowd was sent in advance to the far end of the Esplanade, to the railings, to raise an arm as a signal when the race was over.

The pair stood tensed beside the flagpole. The afternoon was grey and a little breeze blew coldly. Over the whole length of the Esplanade there was only one walker, with a dog, in the middle distance.

'Ready; set; go!' shouted the watch holder, stabbing the air as a signal and setting the second hand moving.

Rosie and Bernard set their jaws and dashed the first few yards, running on the front studs of their skates to pick up the momentum that would hurl them forward. Rosie's steps were shorter and lighter than Bernard's, whose legs ate up the ground. He moved into an immediate lead of half a metre. The ground streamed under them like a river and Rosie felt she was a long way behind.

The running switched to a smooth glide as the two bodies settled into a graceful flow over the asphalt, a purr rising from Bernard's finely-tuned wheels, a clatter from Rosie's.

But Rosie had practised. Every day unless it was raining she was on the Esplanade, striving to improve her rhythm, reduce her time; and now that rhythm came to her aid. Her strides were shorter, more frequent than Bernard's, but her rhythm was perfect. Like relentless pendulums her legs swung, her feet feeling the ground through the clatter of her wheels, never faltering as she forced her body through the air.

They were one quarter of the way over the course . . . one half . . . and gradually the half-metre gap shrank to a few centimetres.

Bernard could skate, there was no doubt; but it was the sheer momentum of his size that carried him on. Now and then an involuntary lurch exposed his poor balance; his legs moved harshly under him and his breath came in uncontrolled gasps. The centimetres were squeezed down to nothing as they ate up the diminishing distance with a rush of wind and a shudder of wheels.

Three-quarters of the way . . . and two metres ahead

of them a woman, elderly and well wrapped, was walking a dachshund. She was travelling in the same direction as Rosie and Bernard, and with her headscarf well forward she could not see them.

They were at her shoulder when Bernard, nearer the low wall than Rosie, altered the angle of his leading foot. The effect was to close off the gap between her and the dog.

The old lady was deaf or deep in thought, for she heard nothing. But the waddling dachshund felt the tremor of their approach through the asphalt and glanced round. The racers were already upon it. Rosie loomed over the dog, skates clattering, wind whistling. The terrified animal hauled itself onto its hind legs, bared its teeth and yapped shrilly.

There was no danger. Although Rosie was trapped between Bernard and the woman, and was bearing down on the dog, she was skilled at avoiding danger. But to avert a collision with the dachshund she could only give ground – a barely discernible change in the rhythm of her stride that allowed Bernard to forge ahead, and gave Rosie room to steer away from the dog.

She choked back her fury, desperate to keep an even flow of breath pumping through her lungs as she cruised in the slipstream that flowed past Bernard's burly frame. She was hypnotized by the rise and fall of his boots, the black wheels scooping up the ground.

Rosie curved aside to find a way past him, and lost yet more ground. Ahead the railings rushed larger and larger. The ligaments in her neck stood out hard as wire as she and Bernard bore down on the girl who was waiting with arm half-raised to signal the finish. They swept up to her, not slowing in the final few metres.

The arm shot up as Bernard plunged by. He curved

round into a clumsy spinning stop followed not one blink behind – but behind all the same – by Rosie. She hurled herself in a slamming, rib-bruising stop against the railings that cut off the four-metre drop to the beach.

She was choking and sobbing; her face burned and the breath scraped in her throat. She wished the railings had not been there so she might plunge over the edge, burying herself in the stones below, blotting out her bitterness and grief.

Behind her the chatter of voices grew as the crowd that had watched them start arrived gasping and running from the far end of the Esplanade.

'One minute fifteen seconds!' shouted a boy, waving the stopwatch aloft. 'Bernard was first!'

The crowd gathered round Bernard.

'Wish I could skate.'

'Must be great.'

'How long you been doing it Bernie?'

'Can you teach me?'

And one voice, as an afterthought, 'Tough luck, Rosie.'

Rosie burst through the group, shamed and bitter and angry. She stood before Bernard who absorbed his triumph, smug and vindicated.

'He cheated!' screamed Rosie. 'He tried to have me over – '

She cut the words off in mid-sentence. They sounded feeble even to her: the whining excuses of a bad loser. There was silence around her. All eyes were on her and there was no sympathy in any of them. They waited.

'That dog . . .' Rosie began again, lamely. The words tailed off. She blushed, staring down at her feet, and in the same view she saw Bernard's feet in their bright, stiff new boots.

11

'If I had boots like that . . .' Rosie breathed, more to herself than to the others; but the words reached Bernard.

'Bad workman blames his tools,' he replied grimly, his lips thin.

Rosie's eyes narrowed, her jaw hardened and jutted and she swung out at him with one foot. The kick missed, and she pivoted around expertly to skate away in the same stride, tearful and flushed.

'I hate you,' she shouted back. 'I hate you all.'

Two

Seven o'clock on a late May morning; crisp and still and bright. Rosie sat on the low wall that divides the Esplanade from the road and watched a lone seagull wheel and dip to a flapping halt high overhead on the flat top of the yacht club flagpole. The bird put its head down and shriek-shriek-shrieked.

Her skates were already on her feet. She had worn them from home, only five minutes away in one of the narrow streets of tightly packed houses in the old part of town. She peeled off her anorak, folded it neatly, and laid it on the wall. She viewed the whole length of the Esplanade westward to the rise of the distant cliffs that held the resort in a curving embrace of red rock. The footpath and the road were deserted except for a milk float purring along the row of seafront houses.

She chose this time because she had a clear run over the entire length of the Esplanade; and because there was no-one to watch her. Since her humiliation with Bernard she couldn't bear to be seen skating by friends from school. Not that she thought of them as friends. She felt alone and angry.

They thought she was the loser, and a bad loser, too. The injustice made her cheeks burn and her eyelids sting. And deep in the dark corner of her mind was the nagging thought that, even if Bernard had not cheated, she might have lost anyway.

She had to win. She couldn't say what drove her; but

13

the next time . . . the next time she had to be first – and she had to be first in less than a minute. She had to be the first person ever to do it. It was desperately important to her. And if the others knew she was practising with such dedication they would want to be in on it, too. The race with Bernard had inspired lots of them, some much older than Rosie.

Roller-skating was becoming a craze. In the past she had made no secret of her dream to her school friends. Some remembered; and they remembered, too, how Rosie shone in the sense of glory of it: breaking a barrier that could never be broken again. People might do it faster afterwards, but no-one could ever again claim that they did it first. The idea appealed to others besides Rosie.

So she practised secretly. She practised before breakfast on schooldays and all day at weekends. If she saw other skaters she drifted idly along, throwing off her air of intense dedication and pretending disinterest. But she gave nothing away.

Sometimes, especially in the afternoons, there would be too many people on the Esplanade to allow room for practice. When that happened she headed for the back streets. They were no use for speed; but she could spin and jump and turn, which helped her become utterly at ease on her skates, so they felt as natural to her as bare feet. They still rubbed and blistered her skin, but the money was growing. With £30 she could buy a new pair; not the best, but good ones all the same, and they would fit her. Then . . . then she would be ready for Bernard.

This was Saturday. Later, if the sun stayed shining, the Esplanade would fill up; but now there was only the seagull and, on the far side of the road, the milkman. She glided to the flagpole and spun in a circle, heels together, toes out, her feet splayed. She turned smoothly to face the length of the Esplanade. She remembered something, went back to the anorak, rummaged in a pocket and pulled out a small alarm clock, furtively, as if she might be stealing it.

It was her mother's. She had, well . . . sort of borrowed it. Her mother didn't know. It had no second hand, but it was the best she could think of with which to time herself.

She could judge by the movement of the minute hand. It wasn't easy, but better than nothing, even if she did feel silly with the bulk of it stuffed in her pocket. She had taken to using it after the race with Bernard, but if there were more than a few people about she never took it out.

She went back to the flagpole carrying the clock. She waited, poised, until it showed exactly 7.15, the minute hand precisely on the three. She sprang forward; dashing, half-run, half-skate, the clock still clutched in her hand, until she achieved enough momentum to switch to the smooth, powerful glide that flung her down the long sweep of the asphalt. Once her rhythm was established she stuffed the clock into her jeans pocket where it bulged uncomfortably.

At the far end one hand went out to absorb the force as she smacked into the railings, while the other hand plunged into her pocket and snatched out the clock. Breathlessly she scrutinized it, trying to make an honest estimate of her performance: was it really nearer a minute and a half, or had the hand travelled only a minute and a quarter, perhaps even less? She refused to cheat herself.

More than a minute and a quarter, she decided, but not much. Her mouth set grimly. She scanned the Esplanade for activity, but there was none. She took a while longer to get her breath and prepared for the return run.

15

And so, as the morning went on, she persisted; hardening herself against the ache in her legs and chest from her efforts. Her sweater was discarded, joining the anorak on the wall.

Gradually the Esplanade came to life: dog-walkers, a couple holding hands, some old people, well wrapped, enjoying the sun on their faces. There were three old people being pushed in wheelchairs, too. There were many homes for the elderly in Sidmouth. It was a favourite place for retirement. When they were no longer able to look after themselves they moved into nursing homes, and a great many such homes had been opened.

Rosie knew some of the old people thought skating was dangerous. On occasions they stopped fearfully as she approached, shrinking within themselves as she sped by. They could not know she was in perfect control. She took care to steer a wide course round them, aware of their fears for their old, fragile bones.

There were many, too, who smiled fondly at her; even stopped to talk to her, envying her age and agility.

This morning though, there was still lots of room. A man was erecting deckchairs in a ribbon of candy stripes along the edge of the Esplanade overlooking the beach. They cut the space down a bit, but Rosie thought she would have an hour or two before the hazards grew too numerous.

Once again she glanced at the clock, waited for the hand to show an exact minute, and shot down the black asphalt path, swerving past a walker, on past a dog and its owner. The dog yapped as she went by. She gave a wide berth to the three wheelchairs and the people pushing them, shaving the low wall at the roadside as she did so. Whizzing by, she heard angry mutterings and knew they were aimed at her. 'Brat!'

'Thoughtless little . . .'

She slowed down as she looked back, and was shocked to see one of those who were pushing shaking his fist at her.

The occupants of the wheelchairs were barely visible: sad little, grey figures drowned in rugs, coats and hats, hardly seeing anything around them. But the drivers, pushing behind, were mouthing fiercely at Rosie. At least, two of them were.

The third was a girl; sixteen, maybe seventeen, whose mouth hung open. She had a vacant look. Rosie sensed without thinking it out that this sad creature was probably a bit simple.

But the other two, muttering bitterly at Rosie's receding figure, were grim and grey.

They were both thin; a man and a woman. He had watery eyes and it was his fist that shook as he mouthed invective against her. He had thin, black hair plastered absolutely flat against his scalp, and big ears. His thin neck stuck out of a drab, grey overcoat. It hardly seemed to touch the collar of his shirt anywhere as it poked through, pale and scrawny.

The woman's face showed nothing. Not, at any rate, by the shape it made about the mouth and jaw. It had a thin mouth; not thin because it was set grimly, as Rosie's sometimes was, but thin by nature. Above it her nose was prominent as a beak, thick and hawk-like. If she walked into a wall, thought Rosie, her nose would touch before anything else. Her hair was black, hacked short and sticking out at all angles, like a badly-used wire brush.

Rosie turned away with a shiver and cruised quickly ahead.

At the railings she didn't bother to look at the clock. She knew the time would be bad. She leaned against the

17

barrier, getting her breath back for another run. She checked the clock, and when the minute hand stood stiffly on the twelve she began again.

It was a good run. Most of the pedestrians had drifted by chance to positions where they gave her a wide, clear strip. She was halfway, blonde hair streaming, when she noticed at the edge of her vision the three wheelchairs.

They were no threat. All three were lined up along the low wall, facing across the Esplanade to the sea opposite a semicircle of stone steps that led down to the beach. The three drivers: the girl, the man and the woman, were behind the wheelchairs sitting on the wall.

Rosie decided to pass on the far side, close to the edge of the Esplanade that dropped to the beach, skimming past the deckchairs and the steps with her head well down to avoid provoking insults.

She was in perfect rhythm, her swinging arms lending extra power to each leg stroke, as she drew abreast the wheelchairs. She did not even see them. She was enjoying the speed and the rhythm as she streamed past, when the man stood suddenly, hands gripping the back of the wheelchair. He shoved it at a running stride ahead of him the short distance to the steps.

The timing was perfect. Rosie was trapped. She was too close, and travelling too fast, to have any chance to swing out behind him. Ahead of her was the wheelchair. In it a grey, frightened face struggled up from the heavy covers, feeble and helpless. To her right were the stone steps. She saw no alternative.

The wheelchair and the old, frightened face were already under her as she forced her legs into a savage swerve. She glanced off the wheelchair footboard, crying out in pain as the corner of it bit into the knob of her

18

ankle bone. She crashed headlong down the stone steps to the beach, scattering the large pebbles as she fell.

Her elbows were sandpapered raw, blood trickled from one knee and her head ached above the right eye. But above all the other injuries her mind was filled with the searing, acid pain of her ankle. Her brain felt filled with ankle, red and blinding, and through gritted teeth and closed eyes the tears began to roll freely. Through them she heard the same shrill voice she had heard earlier.

'You're going to kill someone the way you're going. It's time you were stopped!'

There were traffic noises and the cry of seabirds in the distance, but she could hear none of them; only the thin whining of the voice. She looked up and saw the wheel-chair, and the tall, thin figure behind it, through a curtain of tears. The woman had joined the man and looked down on Rosie from over his shoulder.

Rosie choked back her sobs. 'You – you did it on purpose. I couldn't – I couldn't . . .'

In the wheelchair the grey face was trying to speak. The mouth opened but nothing came out. Rosie looked up at it. 'I'm sorry,' she wept. 'Are you all right?'

The thin man answered for him.

'Oh! Now she's sorry,' he said sarcastically. He looked round for approval, but most of the passers-by were looking at the pale girl lying injured on the pebbles.

He didn't stop. 'Well, it's too late to be sorry,' he snarled. 'Lucky he's not dead.'

He gestured to the figure in the wheelchair. 'Weak heart. Can't take shocks.'

Rosie burned along the whole length of her body. Her ankle was on fire; her knees, elbow and head flamed with pain, but the rest of her seared with shame at the humiliation and injustice.

19

She saw other eyes on her and mistook the frowns of concern for disapproval. She felt utterly alone. She wanted to tell them all she wasn't really like that. She was careful, especially with old people. Instead she let her head drop so her tears fell on to the pebbles of the beach.

There was a scrunch of stones. She raised her head slightly and saw a pair of trainers, battered and grey where they had once been white, with faded blue jeans above them, ragged round the shoes. She looked higher, and above them was a little steel ticket machine on a leather strap that ran up around the neck below a man's face. It was the deckchair man. His eyelids turned down giving him a worried expression, and a frown creased his forehead into multiple lines. He squatted down and put a hand on her shoulder.

'You all right?'

She nodded, thinking at the same time, 'No I'm not. I was cheated.'

'Can you stand?'

She sniffed through the tears and drew herself painfully to her knees. He took her shoulders gently and helped her up. She lifted one leg, easing herself onto the skate, clumsy on the pebbles. She edged the other skate out from under her and straightened her leg. The boot chafed against her ankle and her thoughts flared painfully crimson. She cried out.

'Come and sit down,' he said gently, leading her to a nearby deckchair and holding her weight against him as she eased herself into it.

He turned to the thin man and prodded the air with his forefinger, punctuating his words. 'You're not fit to look after a puppy, let alone an invalid in a wheelchair.'

In the thin face with its slicked black hair the eyes

bulged. The neck rose further out of its collar and the whining voice rose higher still.

'You keep out of it. How dare you. She could've killed us!'

The woman's eyes fixed first on Rosie, then the deck-chair man, before sliding back to Rosie. 'Not now, Gerald,' she hissed in the thin man's ear.

She turned to the girl who was holding back with the other wheelchairs and impatiently signalled her away down the Esplanade. She turned back to Rosie and held her gaze for several seconds, studying her coldly. Then she followed the girl at a stately pace. The man, too, turned away; but not before taking a step back and shaking a fist at Rosie and the deckchair man.

'You'll pay,' he spat. 'You see if you don't!'

He strode away, yanking the wheelchair round, jolting the trembling occupant, and followed the others.

Unpleasant though it had been, the scene had one advantage for Rosie; while she stared, open-mouthed, at his ranting, she forgot a little of her pain and her tears dried up. Now they threatened to return. She whimpered.

The deckchair man knelt beside her and smiled. 'I'm Harry. Hurt still?'

She nodded.

'We better get the skate off.' He looked worried. 'I'll be as gentle as I can. Anywhere else?'

She shook her head, but then added, 'My side, a bit.'

Her hand went to her side and she gasped, 'Oh no!'

'What's the matter?'

Rosie dug into the pocket of her jeans and pulled out her mother's alarm clock. Bits of glass face clinked to the pebbles as they came free of her pocket. The minute hand fell out, too; and as she cradled the clock in her cupped

21

hands the casing fell into two pieces where it had been fractured in the fall. It was quite obviously beyond repair.

'Oh no!' she whispered.

Harry studied her with concern. 'Was it important?'

Tears ran down her lowered face, finding the way to the end of her nose where they dripped onto the broken clock.

'C'mon,' he coaxed. 'It can't be so bad. Tell me. Maybe I can do something.'

In a whisper she explained, coaxed occasionally by Harry, who leaned close to hear her. And the more she told the easier it became, until he had learned about the race with Bernard, the one-minute dream, the need for new boots; everything.

By the time she finished her tears had dried. Harry, whose face became more serious as the story unfolded, knelt silently before her for several moments after she had finished. Then he smiled.

'Well, there's one problem we can fix. Look.' He held up his wrist and showed her a giant watch. Rosie had seen pictures like it. It was the kind divers used, covered in dials and gauges – and it had a second hand that Rosie could see flicking round the face.

'It does everything,' he said. 'And it's everything-proof. So it should be all right – even with you.' He grinned and Rosie managed a small smile back.

'Next time you go skating come and see me. You can borrow it. You might have to strap it higher up your arm to stop it falling off, but it will be easier than stuffing that great thing' – he pointed to the broken clock – 'in your pocket.'

Rosie smiled again. Harry continued: 'But you won't be doing any roller-skating unless you get this seen to.' He lifted her foot gently and she winced.

He finished the task he had begun, carefully releasing the long criss-cross of laces, peeling the worn boot well away from her ankle so he could pull it clear. Blood had oozed through Rosie's white sock.

'Can you move your foot?'

She traced a circle with her big toe, moving the ankle joint through a whole rotation.

'Well, it's not broken. This might hurt a bit.' Still gently, he eased the sock away from the wound and peeled it from her foot. He used the sock to wipe away some of the blood.

'Ankles always bleed a lot,' he said. 'Not much flesh. It's cut, but not too deep. You can't put this back on, though.' He held up the skate. 'Where do you live?'

'Back of the town; not far. Silver Street.'

'Want a lift?'

She hesitated, then shook her head. 'Thank you, no.'

He wrapped the sock into a ball with the bloody part tucked in, and pushed it into the roller boot.

'Might be better if you took off the other one, too. You can walk barefoot.' He helped her unlace it, talking as he did so.

'That was Scribbins; Mr and Mrs. Keep clear of them. They run a nursing home for old people in Ailsa Road. Most people reckon they're barmy. There's some nasty stories going around.

'The oldies go in looking human, and end up looking like the ones they had today: scared out of their wits, and mere skeletons. Rumours are they starve 'em. After today's performance I can believe it.'

He helped her over the pebbles to the steps and she limped up them. He stood watching her from the bottom, hands on hips, smiling widely. 'Don't forget to come and get the watch.'

23

Then he became more serious. 'Good luck with your mum – with the clock.'

'Thank you,' she murmured, and hobbled painfully away.

Three

By the time Rosie reached home the blood had dried on her ankle. There was a graze on her forehead and the tears had run smudged tracks down her cheeks. Her mother's mouth opened in surprise. Intuitively Rosie understood that this was the right moment to declare the clock. With head lowered and a few fresh tears dripping from her nose, she dipped into her anorak pocket and dug out the bits.

'What on earth – ' her mother began. She plucked the shattered clock from Rosie's open hand and dumped it on a kitchen surface. She led Rosie to a chair and sat her down, kneeling before her.

'What happened?'

'I fell down the steps onto the beach. I was tripped.'

Her mother stood, opened a cupboard, lifted down a bowl and filled it with water. She opened a drawer and cut a piece of clean lint from a roll.

'What do you mean, you were tripped? Were you in anyone's way?'

'No, Mum! I was keeping well over and this man pushed a wheelchair right at me. I couldn't help it!'

Her mother was gently swabbing blood from the ankle, but she stopped, looking up sternly.

'A wheelchair! Who was in it?'

'An old man, but – '

'Rosie! You might have hurt him.'

Rosie's voice climbed higher. 'But it wasn't my fault – '

Her mother cut her short. 'I've told you before; if you are going fast, and on wheels, then you are a danger. It's your job to look out. Not everyone else's.

'And what happened to my clock? What were you doing with that? How will I get up? Really – '

'But Mum, you weren't there. Honest; there was this horrible man and his wife. Their name's Scribbins. Everyone knows about them. They run a home and they're cruel to the old people. The man on the beach was telling me – '

'What man?'

'The one who does the deckchairs. Harry. He helped me when I hurt myself. He said no-one liked them – '

'Rosie, stop it! I will not have you talking like that. I've told you before, when there are old people about it's your job to – '

Despite her leg Rosie leapt up, more tears in her eyes, her face flushed. 'It's not fair!' she stormed. 'You never believe me. No-one ever does! You're all horrible!'

She rushed past her mother, knocking the bowl across the kitchen floor, and fled upstairs to her bedroom. Her mother knelt there for a moment or two, staring wearily at the spilled water. With a sigh and a shake of her head she reached for the mop.

The cut on Rosie's ankle kept her off her skates for several days. She amused herself patching the frayed fabric of the boots, strengthening the worn stitching, and oiling the wheel bearings to protect them from the Esplanade grit, borne in on the sea wind.

She was sitting on the step at the back door with a skate between her knees and an oil can in her hand when her mother appeared with the local newspaper, folded open. She thrust it towards Rosie who took it, frowning.

'Read the letter; page seven.' said her mother grimly.

The page was headed: Letters to the Editor. Rosie read: 'Dear Sir, we are sure there are others like us who are sick and tired of the vandals and hooligans who are spoiling life in our beautiful town.

'We have the privilege of looking after some of the old people who come to live the last of their days here. They have all complained bitterly about their fears from the thoughtless youths – boys and girls – who roller-skate on our Esplanade.

'Have they no thought for anyone but themselves?

'I would not have believed it if I had not witnessed it with my own eyes only last week when an extremely ill-mannered girl thundered into us twice in the space of a few minutes.

'Luckily she came to more grief than my patient, but no thanks to her.

'Isn't it time skating was banned altogether on the Esplanade so it can be used by decent people . . .?'

The letter urged the council to change the asphalt for gravel to stop the skaters. It was signed: Gerald and Clarice Scribbins.

Rosie folded the paper quietly and laid it aside. She sensed her mother behind her, and heard her sigh.

'Perhaps that would be the best thing, then we could stop this nonsense for good,' said her mother.

Rosie didn't look up. She had her head in her hands. She knew she was going to carry the blame.

'It wasn't like that, Mum.' She enunciated each word firmly with a kind of desperate patience. 'He did it on purpose. He's horrible. And his wife.' Rosie shuddered at the memory.

'Why?' asked her mother. 'Why would they pick on you – just like that?' She mimicked what she imagined would be Mr Scribbins' voice: 'Oh look, there's a girl skating. I think we'll just try to knock her down with this old man and wheelchair . . .'

Rosie smiled despite herself. Her mother's voices always made her laugh. Her sense of humour defused the conversation and Rosie relaxed a little.

'I don't know,' she said. 'But even Harry thought – '

Her mother held up a hand. 'Enough. Let's not argue any more. But please be careful,' she pleaded. 'There will be a few eyes on you now it's got in the paper.'

Rosie nodded. 'I'm . . . I'm sorry about the clock, Mum.'

Her mother shrugged, smiling and frowning at the same time. 'I'll have to get another one or I'll never get to work on time. But we can't afford it, Rosie. Really we can't. Please be careful.'

Rosie nodded, humbly. 'Can I go skating?'

Her mother nodded, bent down and kissed her daughter briefly. 'Go on. Don't forget . . .'

Together, smiling, they chanted, 'Be careful!'

Rosie walked down to the sea carrying her boots. Her ankle was still sore (but she didn't tell her mother). On the Esplanade she sat near the steps where Harry had the deckchairs stacked, hoping he would see her. It wasn't long before he did.

He walked over, already undoing his watch strap. Grinning, he said, 'Thought they might have cut your leg off. You all right?'

Rosie nodded. 'Thanks for the help.'

He waved it aside and held out the watch. 'Here, I'll help you put it on. Look; if you press this little button it shows seconds. Press it when you stop, and it stops . . . Have you seen the local paper?'

Rosie nodded.

'Best thing you can do is ignore it. Everyone knows Scribbins. They'll know it wasn't quite like that.'

'My Mum believes it.'

'Yes, well . . . Send her down to me. I'll put her straight. Meanwhile I'll keep a lookout for you. Might be best to keep out of their way. Leave your coat. I'll look after it.'

Rosie admired the watch on her wrist. 'This is great, thanks a lot.'

He waved her away, smiling, and watched her cruise along the Esplanade to her starting point at the flagpole.

Rosie was delighted with the watch. On her first run with it she recorded a startling 1 minute 12 seconds! What was more, she knew it was accurate. Eight seconds better than she had previously estimated.

She had started late, so the Esplanade was already filling up with walkers. She decided to make one more pass before she stopped. She would practise in the back streets after that.

Setting the watch she launched herself into a sprint that carried her speeding along the asphalt, sweeping in a wide arc around the occasional pedestrian. She waved to Harry who waved back, grinning as he tore off a ticket for a woman in a deckchair.

She turned back to find a man blocking her path 20 metres ahead, his arms outstretched as if to stop her passing. He was a small man; heavy, but not fat, with fine black hair swept across his shining scalp. He wore a blue suit and he was smiling.

Rosie faltered in her stride. As the distance closed it became obvious that he had his bright, penetrating eyes on her.

'Just a minute, young lady . . .' He began.

Panic swamped Rosie. A sick certainty thickened in

29

the pit of her stomach that this was the work of Gerald Scribbins: a plot to make her suffer. She increased her speed, made to pass on one side of the outstretched arms and as the short, thick body leaned to stop her she feinted away to the opposite side, ducking under the arm towards the flagpole as he called after her, '. . . wanted to talk.'

His voice faded as she sped away.

She was puzzled. He had not seemed angry. He was smiling, and there was no malice in his bright, blue eyes. She idly skated small figures of eight beside the flagpole as she pondered the problem. No answer came to her except that it must be a trap set by Scribbins. Or maybe he was a policeman.

She stopped, worried. It hadn't occurred to her before, but perhaps the police – maybe the council, too – had read the letter in the newspaper and planned to stop the skating. She flushed hotly and the familiar, indignant anger rose up in her, making her brave instead of fearful. She took a deep breath, set her jaw, and took off purposefully back along the Esplanade looking for the small figure in its blue suit.

She was about halfway when she saw him. He was standing beside a pile of deckchairs; and he was talking to Harry. They both watched as she skated nearer. When Harry was certain she had seen them he beckoned to her. The man had a notebook in one hand and a pen in the other.

'Rosie, meet Mr Kitchen,' said Harry. 'He's editor of the local newspaper. Mr Kitchen, this is Rosie.'

The anger went out of her as she watched the two men smiling down at her. Instead she blushed, and backed away a little on her skates, uncertain.

Mr Kitchen held out a hand and beamed: 'Hello Rosie. Nice to meet you. Harry's been telling me about you.'

Rosie took his hand and shook it weakly. 'What did he say,' she said, worried eyes on Harry.

'Have you seen this week's paper? The *Sidmouth Gazette*?' asked Mr Kitchen.

She nodded.

'The letter?'

She nodded again.

'Well, Harry's been telling me his side of it . . . your side really, I suppose. I wondered if you'd tell me about it, too.'

Rosie grimaced. 'No-one's going to believe me. You've already taken their word for it. I'll just get into more trouble.'

Mr Kitchen wagged his pen at her. 'That's not how it works,' he said sternly. 'Mr Scribbins wrote a letter to the editor. He had a point of view and he aired it. Just because we print his letter doesn't mean we're on his side. Mr Scribbins has attacked the roller-skaters and, as I understand it you in particular. Well, I want to hear your side of it.'

'I bet if I'd written a letter you wouldn't have printed it.'

Mr Kitchen frowned. He was silent for a moment, then he said, 'Rosie – I think you're probably right. If you'd written that the owner of a nursing home had tried to knock you over, using a wheelchair patient as a battering ram, I probably wouldn't have printed it.

'And I'll tell you something else: it would have been the wrong decision. Now I'd like to put it right. How about you writing me a letter to the editor?'

Rosie snorted. 'I can't write that kind of letter. It's too . . . I don't know . . . complicated.'

31

'Well, will you tell me about it anyway, and I'll do what I can?'

Harry squatted down beside her. 'Look,' he said. 'Mr Kitchen's all right. Just tell him exactly what happened. No exaggerations or anything. It'll be okay. Trust me.'

Rosie sighed. Harry pulled three deckchairs down and erected them and the trio sat. Mr Kitchen turned to a new page in his notebook. After a pause to collect her thoughts Rosie began.

She started with her arrival at the Esplanade at 7.00 am and went through everything, choosing her words carefully, taking care to be truthful. Sometimes Mr Kitchen wrote down what she said; sometimes he just listened and nodded.

When she finished he asked some questions: how many roller-skaters were there? Why on the Esplanade? Wasn't it dangerous for old people who couldn't move out of the way quickly? Rosie did her best to give good, honest answers.

Finally he closed his notebook and after a pause said: 'Tell me about your one-minute dream.'

She sat upright in her chair, surprised that he knew.

'I told him, Rosie,' said Harry. 'I hope you don't mind.'

Rosie did mind. She felt they were laughing at her and she flushed. She wouldn't look at Mr Kitchen. Instead she scuffed the ground with her skate, 'I don't really want to,' she said moodily.

'Why not?' said Mr Kitchen.

'I don't know,' she shrugged. 'Everyone thinks I'm silly. My Mum doesn't like me doing it. She says it takes up too much time.'

Mr Kitchen stood and the others followed. 'What about a photo?' he said. 'Can I send my photographer to take a picture of you skating along the Esplanade? You can have a copy for yourself.'

Rosie was aghast. 'No way,' she gasped. 'I'm in enough trouble as it is.'

Mr Kitchen beamed at her. 'Young lady,' he said. 'Nonsense! Harry here has told me the wheelchair business was very different from the version in Mr Scribbins' letter, and you've just confirmed every word he said.

'And what's more . . .' He became serious. '. . . I can see for myself. I've seen you lots of times down here skating. It's part of my job to keep my eyes open. And I've got my own ideas about whether you're a hooligan.'

He smiled again. 'If I were you I wouldn't worry too much.'

Harry's hand came out and ruffled her hair, but she ducked away from it, grinning.

'Told you so,' he smiled.

Rosie turned to Mr Kitchen. 'Will you put it in the paper?'

'Wait and see.' He stuffed his notebook into a pocket, his pen in another and held out his hand. Rosie took it.

'Thank you, Rosie. If you change your mind about the photo pop into the office. Everyone calls me Jim. If you ask for Jim they'll fetch me.'

Rosie shook his hand shyly. 'Thank you very much,' she said.

They watched him walk away through the increasing number of pedestrians. Rosie turned to Harry. 'How did he know it was me the Scribbins' letter was about?'

Harry lifted his hands protectively. 'I told him. Are you cross?'

She shook her head.

He said, 'It's just that when I saw what that scrawny pair had written to the paper I got angry. I went to the

33

newspaper office and had a word with Mr Kitchen. He's been keeping an eye out for you since.

'When you didn't turn up for three days I thought something might be wrong. Your ankle, maybe.'

She shook her head. 'It's fine. Mum wasn't too pleased about the clock. She thinks it's all my fault.'

'Well, she'll know differently after next week's paper; if Mr Kitchen puts anything in.'

Rosie was undoing the watch strap. She handed the watch back to Harry. 'Thanks for the loan, but there's too many people now. Can I borrow it again tomorrow?'

'Course.' He tossed her the anorak.

Rosie skated home in high spirits. She traced figures of eight round roadside trees, performed pirouettes, and made death-defying, single-skate runs along the edge of the kerb, pretending that a single slip would send her plummeting thousands of metres to the road below. Really it was only a few centimetres, but she never slipped anyway. She jumped the cracks in the pavements and spun round lampposts.

Things were different now. In half a morning the clouds had lifted from her life. The sun shone. When her mother heard the news she would have to admit it hadn't been Rosie's fault. She gave a yelp of delight, jumped and spun and landed in a perfect glide that brought her to a halt at her front gate.

Her mother was home for lunch. She thrust some sandwiches under Rosie's nose and stuffed one in her own mouth, at the same time shoving clothes into the washing machine and toeing the larder door shut.

Rosie told the whole story of her meeting with Harry and Jim Kitchen, and her mother said, 'Yes, dear,' and 'No, dear,' in more or less the right places. Finally she was struggling into her coat and saying, 'Would you hang

34

the washing out for me when the machine stops, darling. See you later. Be careful – '

'Be careful,' mimicked Rosie, and then in exasperation, 'Oh, Mu-um!' and she slapped her hand down on the table.

Her mother stopped with one foot out of the door. 'What's the matter?'

'You haven't heard any of it!'

'I've been busy, Rosie. It doesn't get done by itself.'

'But it was important!'

'I'm sorry, darling. But I have to hurry, or I'll be late for work. Tell you what, tomorrow I'll bring some sandwiches down to the beach and we'll have them there. How about that?'

Rosie turned the idea over quickly. If she could find a way to make her mother bump into Harry he would tell her what really happened with Scribbins.

'You promise?' she said, guardedly.

'Promise.' Her mother kissed her on the cheek and was gone.

Four

The next day was a grey day. There were breaks in the cloud so that every now and then bright sunlight brought the trees and buildings to life. It did not seem the sort of day for a picnic on the beach. But if the clouds persisted it would be a good day for skating because the pedestrians would stay away.

Rosie dressed, washed, snatched up her roller boots and ran downstairs. Her mother was already making sandwiches.

'It might clear up, but if it doesn't you'll have to come home for lunch.'

Rosie grabbed an apple.

'That won't do. You eat a proper breakfast.'

'Not hungry,' she called back as she went through the door. The last thing she heard her mother call was, 'Be careful . . .'

Although it was early, Harry was already on the beach sorting out deckchairs that needed repairs. His big hands held three at once, and he raised them with ease above his broad back, carrying them to a car and trailer at the roadside. He grinned when he saw her and began unfastening his watch strap.

'You're keen. Going to break any records today?'

'Don't know.' She let him fasten the watch on her wrist. 'Will you be here at lunchtime?' she asked.

He looked at the sky. 'Unless it rains. No-one wants deckchairs in the rain. Why?'

'My mum's coming down; bringing a picnic. Will you tell her about Scribbins? Like you did with Mr Kitchen? Please?'

Harry smiled. 'Pleasure,' he said.

Rosie skated. The wind was strong, and quite cold when the sun went behind a cloud. She kept her anorak on. Skating away from the yacht club the wind was against her and her times were poor. And her feet hurt from the pinching boots, so she was unable to beat, nor even to match her previous day's time of 1 minute 12 seconds.

Still, there was room to skate, and she was happy. Some schoolfriends appeared, also on skates. This time Rosie didn't leave. They, too, had heard about the newspaper letter. One of them asked, 'Was it you – that got in Scribbins' way?'

She nodded. The others were silently impressed. 'What's he like? Were you frightened?'

So Scribbins did have a reputation in the town, she thought. Harry was right. Maybe people wouldn't blame her. She sensed, too, that her friends stood in awe of her conflict with the grim, grey Scribbins.

''Course not,' she lied.

'Pity you didn't run him over,' said one. 'He's awful. He lives just up the road from me. My dad says he poisons the old people.'

Another added: 'Mc and Gillian have heard his missis shouting at 'em lots of times.'

'And the girl they've got working there – you know, the daft one – she's always crying. She's terrified of 'em.'

In the heat of gossip they forgot Rosie and she continued with her skating. The day remained cloudy, but the patches of blue grew larger and more frequent. A few people were venturing out. An old lady was being pushed in a wheelchair (but not by Scribbins). The wind was dying. Rosie felt a ripple of . . . expectation? . . . creep up her spine; like a secret message from inside herself that the day was going to be special in some way. Maybe she would cut some more time off her record. That would be good; especially if her mother and Harry were there to see it.

She was smiling as she skated and, looking up, she caught the eye of an old man in a wheelchair who was watching her quizzically. When he saw her smile he smiled back out of brown eyes buried deep in a wrinkled, walnut-brown face. He had a moustache that was grey to its roots and it was impossible to see his mouth under it.

His scalp was as brown as his face, covered in a few strands of grey hair that could not protect it from the sun, and he seemed overwhelmed by the wheelchair and the size of his overcoat and the rug that covered his knees.

Rosie liked him, and as she continued on her way her smile broadened and she gave him a little wave, only half sure of herself.

He was still there when she returned, and this time he was smiling so widely she could even see his mouth. He clapped his hands quietly as she passed. She returned a brief, shy smile as she sped by, and once beyond him she beamed with warmth and happiness.

Her time was not a good one because she hadn't been concentrating. But she didn't care; the clouds were parting, the Esplanade was virtually empty, she had some friends again. With a quick glance at the watch and an inward laugh of delight she flew down the Esplanade.

Once again she drew close to the spot where the old man had been watching; but this time when she looked up he was no longer waiting at the side of the Esplanade. The wheelchair was edging its way into her path. The wheels had an extra outside rim and by grasping them the frail old man was pushing himself forward with surprising strength.

Rosie faltered and slowed, all the warmth draining out of her as a vivid picture came back of her last unhappy encounter with a wheelchair.

Her heart was slamming against the wall of her chest. Quickly she looked around . . . beyond the old man in his wheelchair . . . on to the beach. There was no sign of Scribbins. She could see Harry further ahead handing over tickets to customers, but he was too far away to hear if she cried out.

She calmed a little as she reasoned that, whatever this old man had planned, it was badly timed. She had room to slow down; to stop, even. So there could be no damage done.

The old man was still beaming. His hands were once again clapping softly.

Rosie was puzzled.

'Bravo, miss! Bravo!'

Her eyes grew wide and the tension that had engulfed her evaporated. He just wanted to be friendly!

His voice seemed like an impossible voice for such a frail body. It was firm and clear and had none of the tremulousness of most old people. Her mouth dropped open. Her confusion must have shown for the old man said, 'Close your mouth. Close your mouth; you look like a simpleton, miss. A simpleton, hm?'

Rosie's mouth drew slowly shut and her eyes grew wider to compensate.

'You look more charming when you smile, miss. Much.' He held a hand out to her. 'Well, come along. Shake my hand. Shake my hand, hm?'

She shook it weakly.

'Good; good. Permit me to introduce myself. My name

is Jackson. Charles. I have others in between, but those will do. And you?'

'Er . . . I've only got two,' replied Rosie, baffled. He had so much energy. Despite her feeble handshake he had pumped her arm vigorously. And she felt that all the energy that was trapped in the confines of the wheelchair was pouring out with controlled power through his voice.

He 'tutted' several times. 'Of course; of course. We've all got at least two, miss. But what are they, pray? What are they? Hm?'

'Er . . . Rosie. Rosie Swallow.'

'Excellent. Excellent. And how old are you Rosie?'

'Eleven, sir. Nearly twelve.' Her brain was recovering from the surprise. She relaxed as she sensed there was no trap. She was surprised she had called him sir. She wouldn't normally think of it, but somehow it seemed impossible to call this old man anything else.

'Twelve, eh? Well now, miss. That makes me nearly seventy years your senior. Seventy years, mind. So I think we'll proceed like this: I shall call you Rosie. May I call you Rosie? How about it? Hm?'

Rosie nodded lamely.

'And you shall call me Mr Jackson. Later, when we get to know each other better, we will see; but for now it will be Mr Jackson. Is that acceptable, Rosie?'

He was still beaming at her, and Rosie could not help beaming back. His funny, clipped, repetitive way of speaking might have sounded stern from the wrong face, or in different circumstances; but on this particular day, coming from this small, brown, beaming face it was warm and welcoming.

She laughed lightly and said, 'Yes, sir.'

'Mr Jackson.'

'Yes, Mr Jackson.'

40

'Well, don't you have any questions, Rosie?'

Rosie was bewildered. She had hundreds; but she couldn't get them to take shape and come out of her mouth. She shrugged and shook her head instead.

Mr Jackson laced his fingers into one another on his lap. 'Don't you want to know what on earth I'm talking about, hm?'

Rosie grinned. 'Well, yes . . . I suppose I do.'

He indicated the low wall that separated the Esplanade from the roadway. 'Let's sit down. I don't have any choice, but you'll be more comfortable, hm?'

He wheeled himself close to the wall and turned his chair to face the sun. Rosie sat beside him. He cleared his throat. 'Well now, I can see you like skating. Watched you. Been staying at that hotel.'

He indicated a seafront hotel overlooking the Esplanade a few yards from the yacht club.

'Good; good. Fine sport. Keep you fit. But you – you, Rosie, don't merely like it. You adore it. You are dedicated to it, hm? Why else would you be out here at seven o'clock every morning. I've been watching.

'So . . . what's it all about, miss? Why so keen, hm?'

Rosie felt the flush of embarrassment. Her toes squirmed in her boots. Her one-minute dream was personal. More and more people were getting to know and she wasn't too happy about spreading it any further.

'I don't know,' she hedged. 'I just like going fast.'

'Hmmm?' Mr Jackson eyed her narrowly, thinking; then dismissed the question and twisted to look along the Esplanade, first one way, then the other. 'How long is this path?'

She replied without hesitation. 'Four hundred and ninety one metres, thirty eight centimetres.'

41

'And how fast can you skate it, hm? I've watched you timing yourself.'

Rosie couldn't help herself. The words flooded out of her like a dam bursting. 'Once, ages ago, I did it in one minute ten seconds. But that didn't really count because it was blowing a gale and the wind was behind me and I had to count it out myself because I didn't have a clock. But now someone's lent me a watch and the best time I've done is one minute twelve seconds. I could do it faster but my skates are getting small. I've nearly got the money for some better ones and when I get them . . .'

She paused, seeing in her mind the day when she would live the one-minute dream. She could see the flags and the cheering and the band. She knew it wouldn't be like that really, but it felt like it in her dream.

If she could do it . . . No, when she did it . . . she would feel like an Olympic champion, and it wouldn't matter if it was six o'clock in the morning and there was no-one to see it but a curious seagull and an indifferent cat.

'. . . when I get them I'm going to do it in under one minute.' She paused again and breathed to herself almost silently, '. . . under one minute.' And the light shone in her eyes.

Mr Jackson smiled and said triumphantly, 'Aha! Aha, so that's it, hm? Under one minute. And it's one minute twelve seconds now, hey? Well, that's a lot to take off, no doubt about it. But you can do it. Of course you can.'

He stopped, and looked at her keenly. 'May I help you Rosie, hm?'

She didn't know what to say. She wanted to ask: How? You're stuck in a wheelchair; but it would have sounded rude. He watched as her eyes were drawn to the blanket that covered his legs and he guessed what was going through her mind.

'Let me tell you about myself.'

He waved a hand dismissively at his legs. 'They just won't work. Don't know why. Been getting worse for years; and here I am. Stuck, hm?

'But . . . but, Rosie, when I was your age I used to roller-skate myself. And I was the only one, y'know. Only one. It wasn't popular then.

'They didn't look like yours, though. Oh, no. You couldn't buy them in those days; d'you see? My father made the first ones. They tied on to my shoes with string. Very hard work they were, too. Very hard. But then he modified them; better wheels, leather straps. Started making them for friends, too.

'They couldn't beat me, though. Practising every spare minute. Like you, hm? But it still wasn't fast enough. Then I got older; started studying the whole thing. Not just the skates mind. Me too. How my legs worked; the best way to get maximum speed from them; all that sort of thing.

'For instance, I've been watching you.' He stood his fingers on his lap like two matchstick legs, illustrating as he spoke. 'Your feet are pushing backwards and out-wards, like this.' He showed her with his fingers.

'If you put more effort into the backward push, like this . . . then you won't waste so much energy. You'll go faster.' He waved her away. 'Go on. Go on; try it, hm?'

She was bewildered. 'But – '

'No buts, miss. I have a watch. Just you concentrate. More backward power, remember. I'll time you from the flagpole to the far end. Go on; go on.'

She did as he said, overwhelmed by his energy.

When she got to the flagpole she looked up at him. He

43

was studying his watch, one arm raised in the air. She poised, her eyes fixed on him, ready to spring forward. The hand sliced down and she was off.

He was right; her legs were thrusting not only backwards, but at a sideways angle as well. She had never thought of it before. She tried to make them push backwards. It seemed to help.

Already she was abreast of him and he called out as she sped by, 'Head down – wind resistance!'

It was all she heard before she was out of earshot, streaming through the wind. She crouched lower over her skates, and forgot about her legs. They began to slide out sideways again. She remembered and corrected. Head down, body low, legs thrusting out behind; she wasn't even aware of the ground under her.

Suddenly she had reached the far end. She slammed into the railings, winded. When she had got her breath she cruised quickly back to join Mr Jackson. He was beaming broadly. 'One minute ten seconds,' he cried triumphantly. 'You see, hm?'

Rosie lifted her head and laughed; a bright peal of musical laughter that turned the few heads that were in earshot. She felt like throwing her arms round him, but didn't dare.

'Thank you,' she grinned. 'Thanks a lot.'

'Good heavens! That's nothing. Just an example. I'll tell you something else, hm? You must use your arms more. Pump with your arms. Good for the breathing, help establish a rhythm, push you forward. No, no, no. Don't do it now. Sit down. Sit down, I haven't finished yet.'

Rosie resumed her seat on the wall.

'Where did I get to, hm? Oh yes; my old skates: Well, I got faster and faster; but it still wasn't enough. Then I thought about the skates. I talked to my father and together we built a new pair. Different wheels, see?' He adopted a conspiratorial tone and leaned towards her. 'It's in the axles, Rosie. The bearings and the axles, hm? You'll never believe the difference they made. It was like flying. The bearings were as nearly perfect as it is possible to be. They floated in oil as softly as a bubble floating. No friction d'you see, Rosie? Friction is what holds you back. Nothing could hold me back but the wind.' The old eyes glinted with excitement. 'It was like flying, Rosie. Like flying. No friction, d'you see?'

Rosie wasn't sure she did see. They had studied friction a little bit at school. She remembered the word. If it had anything to do with skating faster she wished she had listened.

She nodded anyway, as a gesture that he should go on. His eyes were unfocused, somewhere in the middle distance where the days of his boyhood hung. He was silent a while longer, then quietly, seriously, he said, 'I still have those skates, Rosie. Kept them polished and oiled. All these years they have been my prized possession. How would you like them, hm?'

Rosie's mouth dropped open.

Mr Jackson grinned. 'You are doing it again, miss. Kindly close your mouth. What's your answer? What d'you say, hm?'

She flushed. 'I couldn't. They – they must be special. I mean . . . you know . . .' she paused. 'And . . .'

'Go on,' he urged.

'It's just that, well, I want to do it myself. Me. Rosie Swallow. I don't want it to be because I had a special advantage. I mean, I could have jet skates, couldn't I? I don't mean it rudely Mr Jackson, honestly, but . . .'

Mr Jackson was laughing. 'Just right. Just right. Knew

45

you were my kind of girl soon as I saw you. That's the right attitude. I'm impressed.' He winked at her. 'But think of this: look at your skates. Are they the best skates, hm?'

'No; but soon I'll have the money to get better ones.'

'Aha! You see? You don't think it's cheating to get better ones, do you? Of course not. It isn't. But mine are the best. The very best, hm? They might be old,' his eyes glinted again, 'but they are without doubt the best in the world, in the universe! But it's still up to you. You are the skater: they won't go, Rosie Swallow, unless you make them go. What d'you say, miss; hm?'

'I couldn't take them, Mr Jackson. It wouldn't be right,' she stammered. 'You – you've had them for so long; and they're special. You mustn't give them away.'

He frowned, thoughtfully. 'Tell you what then. You borrow them. You borrow them and let me be your trainer; your coach. And we'll see how we get on. How about that, hm?'

Rosie's smile gradually spread over her face into a grin that lifted her ears.

'Shake hands on it,' the old man said, holding his out. Rosie took it and he pumped it vigorously.

'How long are you here for?' she asked.

'For good. I shall be living here from now on. I have no family and I can no longer manage on my own. I have always been fond of Sidmouth. I have decided to live here until I die. And I am delighted to have found something enjoyable to do in the meantime. I was afraid it was going to be boring.'

'I thought you said you were staying at a hotel?'

'So I am, but as soon as I find a suitable retirement home I shall move into it.

'Now, in the meantime miss, I am tired; and it is nearly

46

my lunchtime. Therefore I shall return to my hotel for lunch and a nap. I look forward to seeing you here again tomorrow. What time do you propose, hm?'

Rosie's face dropped. 'It's school tomorrow. I won't be able to come until after that. About four thirty.' Her face dropped further. 'And if it's crowded there won't be room.'

'That would be a pity, but we will see. I shall be here unless it is raining. You'll need to bring some plimsoles.'

'Plimsoles? What are plimsoles?'

'You know; tennis shoes, hm?'

'Oh, you mean trainers.'

'Is that what they call them now? Very well, bring some trainers.'

Rosie stood up. 'Can I help you back to the hotel?'

'No need, thank you. A young man from the hotel is collecting me at twelve thirty and I see . . .' He looked at his watch, '. . . it is that now.'

He looked along the Esplanade. 'And here he comes. Admirable punctuality.'

He turned to Rosie and said: 'Well, miss; I am delighted to make your acquaintance. Until tomorrow . . .' He beamed at her broadly and wheeled himself away towards a uniformed young man who approached from the hotel.

Rosie watched as the young man moved into place behind the wheelchair and took control. Mr Jackson leaned round the back of it and gave one last wave. Rosie returned it.

She stood for some minutes reflecting on the previous half hour. Already it felt as if it had been a dream. But there was the old man being wheeled away. He had spoken to her; he had shaken her hand; and he was going to help her.

This strange, fierce, beaming old gentleman – he was obviously a gentleman – was going to help her fulfil the one-minute dream!

With a whoop she did a pirouette on one skate and shot off down the Esplanade, concentrating on keeping her head down, her body low and her legs thrusting directly out behind as he had instructed. She was sure she could feel the extra speed.

Harry was standing behind the long line of candy-striped deckchairs handing out tickets as she approached him. He waved, and she waved back. It was then that she remembered her mother, who was bringing a picnic lunch to the beach.

She looked at Harry's watch. It was 12.45. Her mother should have been there already. Rosie was afraid she might have missed her – which would mean no lunch and a lecture later – when she spotted her parking their battered old car further down the Esplanade.

Rosie skated level as her mother gathered up her handbag and the sandwich bag, locked the car and crossed to meet her.

'Sorry I'm late.' She kissed her daughter on the fore-head. 'They've got the whole of Fore Street dug up and everyone has to make a detour. Even the bicycles. Why do they do these things when the tourist season is just about to start?'

Rosie grabbed her free hand and tugged. 'Come and meet Harry. He's lent me his watch to time myself by.'

She didn't mention Scribbins. She thought it would be best if he brought it up.

Harry was still at the deckchairs. Rosie introduced

them and he made a generous theatrical bow, punched two tickets from his machine and offered them. 'Charmed I'm sure,' he said. 'Have a seat.'

Rosie's mother flushed and smiled. 'I'm afraid it's the pebbles for us. No money.'

'Madam, you do me an injustice.' He bowed again. Rosie laughed. Harry continued, still holding out the tickets. 'These are with my compliments. Please . . .' He gestured towards the deckchairs.

'But what will your boss say?' asked Rosie's mother.

Harry put his hand on his chest and said, 'I am he. All this . . .' He swept an arm along the length of the deckchairs, '. . . is mine. And this.' He held up the ticket machine. 'And over in the car park I have a seven-year-old Ford with rust, and a trailer behind. And that is absolutely everything I own in the world.'

He dropped the theatrical pose and added: 'So – if I say you can sit, you can sit. And I hope you'll feel free any time.'

Rosie's mother said, 'It's very kind of you; and I will this time if,' she stressed the word, 'if you will have lunch with us. It's only sandwiches and some cake.'

He leapt into a deckchair and held out his hands. 'Done!' They all laughed again.

'I'll be back in a minute,' said Rosie. 'I'm just going to have one more skate.'

'Well I like that,' gasped her mother. 'I've done all these for her.' She indicated the sandwich bag.

'My gain,' said Harry. 'She'll be back. How's her ankle now?'

'Her ankle?'

'From the fall the other day. Not that you could call it a fall. Definitely not her fault . . .'

They were in conversation. Rosie made one pass along

the Esplanade, then another, and another. She kept one eye on Harry and her mother, who barely raised their heads as they talked.

The sky had changed. The clouds had broken up into occasional grey rags. Most of the time the sun shone warmly.

She guessed her mother would be learning the truth about her battle with the Scribbinses and she intended to give Harry plenty of time to tell it all. Half an hour later she returned to them, just as her mother rose.

'I had no idea it was so late,' she was saying. 'I have to go. I've got things to do.'

Rosie stood with her hands on her hips, indignant. 'What about my sandwiches?'

Her mother put a hand to her mouth and looked first at Harry, then at the bag. 'I think we've eaten them all.'

Rosie was about to howl when Harry spun a coin high in the air. Rosie caught it. 'Don't panic,' he said. 'There's two left and you can buy an ice cream as well; if you get one for me. You want one, Kate?'

Rosie's mouth dropped open for the umpteenth time that day. It was 'Mrs Swallow' half an hour ago. Now it was 'Kate'.

'No thanks,' said her mother. 'No time. See you tomorrow.'

'See you tomorrow?' Rosie looked up at Harry as she waved goodbye to her mother. 'What does that mean?'

'She's bringing lunch down to the beach again.'

'But I'm at school.'

He looked at her, grinning, and caught her neck in the crook of his arm, pulling her head into him affectionately. 'Who said anything about you?'

She squirmed free with a snort and sped off to the ice

50

cream kiosk. She took an ice cream back to Harry. The Esplanade was filling up in the sunshine. She decided to stop skating for the day. She gave Harry his watch, thanked him and set off with her ice cream for home.

Her mother had been right. Fore Street was completely shut off. There were barricades and mechanical diggers and the road was covered with rubble. No good for skaters. She went the long way round.

Later that evening while Rosie cleaned her skates and her mother was ironing, singing softly while she worked, Rosie said, 'I hear you're having lunch with Harry.'

'What? Oh, yes dear.'

'What about me?'

'You'll be at school.'

'But he's my friend; not yours.'

Her mother bent down and kissed her on the nose. 'You have very good taste.'

Rosie rubbed the kiss away, squirming. 'What did you talk about today?'

'Oh, lots of things.'

'Did he talk about me?'

'Of course. He said you were very nice – '

Suddenly her mother remembered. She stood the iron in its stand and squatted in front of the chair in which Rosie was sitting, hands on Rosie's knees.

'And he told me he saw exactly what happened with Scribbins,' she kissed Rosie. 'I'm sorry. You were right, it seems.'

She looked quizzically at her daughter, studying her shrewdly. 'Is that why you wanted me to go down there?'

Rosie concentrated on cleaning a skate wheel. 'No,' she lied. 'I just thought you might like to meet him.'

'You were right. Thank you.'

51

'Couldn't I skip school dinners and have lunch with you two, then; down at the beach?'

Her mother had gone back to the ironing; but she held the iron hovering in mid-air as she stared absently into the wall opposite.

'Certainly not . . .' she said.

Five

Next day at school Rosie was more her old self. She had forgotten her humiliation in the race with Bernard. Too much else had happened. And the other children were eager to hear of Rosie's battle with Mr and Mrs Scribbins.

Her excitement at the meeting with the strange, beaming, abrupt old Mr Jackson came bubbling out at morning break. She told a thick circle of friends how he had offered her a pair of special skates that would make her faster than anyone (Bernard snorted, 'Anyone can win if they've got better skates!' and Rosie generously ignored him).

Through lessons she whispered the story of her conversation with Jim Kitchen from the newspaper; and by afternoon break the tale about the Scribbinses had reached the proportions of a major horror film. Rosie watched her spellbound audience and allowed her imagination room to stretch. She was enjoying the attention.

But although her tongue ran away she was careful to keep her secrets. She never mentioned any of the advice Mr Jackson had given her on improving her skating. Locked away inside her was a determination to show she was the fastest of them all. No-one was going to rob her of the one-minute dream.

After school she planned to head straight for Mr Jackson on the Esplanade instead of home. The weather was fine and she had her trainers as he had instructed.

She was walking out through the schoolgates when a group of classmates stopped her, led by Bernard.

The big boy smiled. 'Rosie, could we come and watch?'

'Please?' said another.

'We won't say anything. We'd just like to see the skates.'

Rosie's thoughts hardened as she listened. This was the price she paid for talking. They were asking now, but if she refused they would probably go along anyway. The Esplanade was a public place, after all. Better, she thought, to give in gracefully. And anyway, just seeing the skates couldn't do any harm. There was only one pair and Mr Jackson was lending them to her.

She nodded. 'Don't get in the way, though. He's an old man. He doesn't want lots of mucking around.'

The group cheered and Bernard said, 'Thanks.'

When they arrived at the Esplanade Mr Jackson was already there, wrapped in his overcoat and rug despite the warmth of the sun. On his lap he held a bundle; the outer wrapping was a faded, grimy green cloth. He looked at his watch.

His eyes were twinkling, but there was no smile under his moustache. 'It is 4.35 pm, Miss Rosie Swallow. 4.35 pm. I have been waiting here five minutes. A true athlete must know the meaning of time. Who are these young people?'

He surveyed the peering, wondering mob of heads.

'I'm sorry I'm late, Mr Jackson. But they all wanted to come. They stopped me at the school gates. I hope you don't mind.'

'Hm. Well, perhaps not. We shall see. Have you got your trainers?'

She held them up.

'Well then; get them on; get them on. Be sure you tie

them tightly. You will need to strengthen your ankles because, unlike the skates you are used to, these will not give you sufficient ankle support.'

As he spoke he unwound the green cloth. Inside it was another bundle made like a wallet with two pockets. From the pockets he drew first one skate, then the other.

Rosie was horrified. From the group behind her there was a series of stifled snorts.

Mr Jackson proudly held up one of the skates. There was almost nothing to see. The skate was a bare skeleton of metal with four black rubber wheels attached. The steel frame looked as if it had been cut by hand with a hacksaw (which, indeed, it had). There was a half moon of metal across the front edge designed to hold the toe of a shoe. The back and front wheels were on separate sections, held together by a wingnut on a sliding bar. On the back section was a raised edge to hold the heel. At back and front there were two wide, stiff leather straps with heavy buckles which secured the skates to the shoes of the wearer.

Rosie felt the colour rise up her neck and into her ears and cheeks. They were no better than the skates that little children wore. Beginners' skates! No; they were worse than that. Even beginners' skates were shiny, with brightly coloured wheels, chromed nuts, coloured straps. These skates of Mr Jackson's were . . . homemade!

Sniggers had broken out behind Rosie. She burned with embarrassment, not only for herself but for Mr Jackson. He was over 80 years old. She should have realized he could have no idea how sophisticated roller boots had become.

She felt sorry for him. Humiliated though she was, she could not bear the idea of this beaming old man being laughed at.

'Get 'em on, Rosie,' someone sniggered. 'He can pull you behind the wheelchair.'

A chorus of jeers followed. Mr Jackson was studying Rosie. He was looking for a sign that she shared his pride in the old skates, but he found none. His gaze moved to the group behind her and all he observed was their mockery. He was puzzled. Another voice called from behind, 'Just sit on his lap. It'll be quicker.'

Rosie's lip curled. With a snarl she turned on the crowd, lashing out everywhere. But they knew about Rosie's temper, and as she flailed to left and right they were already scattering across the Esplanade, screaming and giggling.

'Rosie!' Mr Jackson's hard, strong voice stung them all into stillness. It hung in the air as Rosie stood with her eyes to the ground, an angry tear forming in the corner of one eye.

He wheeled himself forward until he was level with her, gripped her elbow and turned her towards him.

'Look at me.'

She wouldn't. He shook the elbow. 'Look at me.'

She raised her eyes to his. The scattered children began to re-form in twos and threes, but stayed a little distance off.

'What on earth is going on, miss. Hm?' His eyes were gentle and concerned. They made Rosie want to cry all the more.

'I'm sorry, Mr Jackson. I just don't know why they have to be so . . . so horrid!' She spat the last two words out vehemently, turning her angry gaze on the distant children as she did so.

'Was it to do with the skates?'

She nodded, not able to look at him.

'What's wrong with them?'

56

'Nothing's wrong with them; really,' she lied. 'They just look a bit, well . . . old.'

He beamed up at her. 'Of course. Of course, my dear. About seventy years old, in fact.'

'Yes. But you see . . . we don't wear skates like that any more.' She added gently. 'They aren't even made, you know, properly.'

He laughed out loud. Heads craned to hear from the distance. 'Homemade, you mean? Yes, well . . . I know what you mean. Know what you mean. Didn't matter so much when I was a lad, hm?' He leaned towards her, lowering his voice. 'Trust me, Rosie. Trust me. These old, homemade skates are better than any skates anywhere in the world. They are better than the most modern, most expensive, shiniest, professional skates you can buy today, no matter what the price. No matter what!

'It's all in the bearing, you see. In the bearing,' he stressed. 'And that's the bit no-one can see. The rest of the skate doesn't matter a jot. Not a jot. See? Hm?'

Rosie didn't, but she nodded anyway. He held up a skate and asked, 'What would happen if you held up one of your skates like this and spun the wheel?'

She frowned, puzzling to understand what he was driving at. 'The wheel would spin, I suppose.'

'Yes, yes; of course. The wheel would spin. And then what?'

'Well, then it would stop.'

'Quickly? Slowly?'

'Quite quickly, I suppose; why?'

Mr Jackson put a finger to the side of his nose, and winked. 'Take this.' He handed her the skate.

'Now, spin one of the wheels. Go on, a good hard spin.'

Behind her the others were straining unsuccessfully to see and hear what was happening.

Rosie put her thumb against the wheel and set it spinning forcefully. Nothing seemed to happen. She could hear nothing and the wheel appeared not to be moving. She put out a finger, tentatively, to test it.

'Wait!' commanded Mr Jackson. 'Hold it near your face. Not too near. You'll feel it.'

Rosie held the wheel near her cheek and felt the faint breath of wind from the spinning surface. At that distance, too, her ears picked up the faintest murmuring hum. She held the skate where she could watch it, and the fascination of it was like a magic that made her hold her breath. The wheel was spinning; of that she had no doubt now. But it was so perfectly balanced on its axle that the movement couldn't be seen, nor heard, except up close by the little eddies of wind it created.

She thought of her own skates that clattered and shuddered as they spun. Even the best skates, better than the ones she planned to buy, could be seen and heard perfectly clearly.

'It's amazing,' she breathed.

'It hasn't finished yet,' said Mr Jackson, watching spellbound, too.

They both waited. The wheel kept spinning. Rosie held it to her face again to check. It had been spinning for half a minute and showed not the slightest sign of slowing. It spun and spun, and Rosie's eyes grew wider and wider. A minute passed. Rosie gasped, unbelieving, 'It's still not slowing down.'

The wheel went on, noiseless, unseen; the movement untraceable except close against the sensitive skin of Rosie's cheek where she could feel the breath of wind.

She looked at Mr Jackson grinning back at her and she cried, 'It's magic!'

'No, Rosie,' he laughed. 'Not magic; but aren't you

58

amazed? It's science. It's my own secret formula that no-one in the world knows but me; and you shall help me test it, hm?

'Can you imagine what will happen when you put those on your feet? I know they look old and badly put together; but Rosie, they are the nearest thing to absolutely friction-less wheels the world has ever seen.

'They will stop, of course, eventually. But it takes ages. Ages and ages and ages.' He was wriggling with excitement in his wheelchair.

Rosie held the skate up to her face again. She fancied she could feel a slight change in the whisper of wind against her cheek, as if the wheel were slowing down. It was minutes since she had set it spinning.

'Try them on,' urged Mr Jackson.

She sat on the wall and held one skate against the bottom of her trainer, loosened the wingnut and slid the two parts until they fitted her foot, then tightened the nut again. She buckled the straps tightly over her forefoot and round her ankle. She did the same with the other.

Mr Jackson warned, 'Remember, these skates are not like the ones you are used to. These wheels float on their bearings like a bubble in air. If you are not careful they will soon have you off your feet. Mark my words, miss.'

Rosie eased herself gently into an upright position. She felt as if she was standing afloat in oil; as if the skates were waiting for a chance to slide, quick as sunlight, from under her. She stood with her arms out clumsily, alert to the knowledge that these skates were alien to her. Old and ill-fitting as her own skates were, she was rarely aware of their presence on her feet; she had become a part of them, them of her.

But she knew that until she had spent many hours in

these skates with their smooth, humming beauty, they could be lethal. She cautiously moved one foot.

'Want to hold my hand,' called a voice from the watching children. A peal of derision went up.

'Ignore them,' ordered the old man, firmly. 'Concentrate.'

But it was too late. Rosie turned only her head to face the direction of the taunt, but it was enough. The sudden movement altered her balance and before she could compensate the frictionless wheels had slid away from under her. The skates rushed forward and kicked up. Her whole body fell heavily backwards.

She heard the whoop of laughter from her unwelcome spectators and the sharp, alarmed 'Rosie!' from the old man, before she hit the ground on her back with a shuddering crunch that jarred the base of her spine and sent a searing pain through her neck as her head snapped sharply backwards.

The wheels of the skates spun noiselessly on and on as Rosie lay wincing. The watching children doubled their bodies, helpless with laughter, supporting each other weakly in their amusement.

The pain eased. Rosie shifted onto her side. Mr Jackson had wheeled himself closer and laid a hand gently on her shoulder. Rosie rubbed her neck. As the pain subsided she became aware of the world around her: the hand on her shoulder, traffic, seagulls – and the jeering children.

Her eyes blazed, and in one smooth movement she pulled herself round and upright, holding on to the wheelchair for support. No-one saw her pluck a stray pebble off the ground as she rose. Mustering all her strength she hurled it into the braying group.

Had she thrown it from a more stable platform her aim might have been more accurate, the stone may have travelled with greater speed. As it was one of them saw it coming.

'Look out!' he screamed. The laughter ceased abruptly and the children parted as the stone cleared a path between them and clattered harmlessly down the empty Esplanade, ricocheting onto the beach.

There was silence. The two groups studied each other in sullen animosity. Everyone, everything, held its breath. The seagulls and the traffic, even the wind, seemed to be waiting . . .

Mr Jackson spoke first, addressing the crowd of school children. His eyes blazed with the familiar intense light and a daunting fierceness. 'So . . . it missed you. You are luckier, perhaps, than you deserve, hm? And you are also ill-mannered. I suggest you go and find something else to do. Somewhere else. Please do not bother us again.'

Silently, truculently, in small groups they began to disperse. The old man turned to Rosie. Still there was no humour in his eyes. It contained a brightness, but it was not the humorous shine Rosie loved, only a glint. 'Your temper is not acceptable, young lady; hm? You have spirit, and I admire spirit. But there is no room for temper. Temper will destroy you. Spirit will help you triumph.

'Look at me, Rosie Swallow. Come . . . look at me.'

Rosie's mouth was down at the corners, her eyes were hard. Reluctantly she raised her eyes to his.

'You may sulk,' he conceded. 'Nevertheless you *will* listen. I cannot help you if you cannot contain your temper. This is the last time. Do you agree? Hm? Do you?'

Rosie nodded, the sulk giving way to misery.

'Promise?'

She nodded again.

61

He squeezed her arm. 'Well, I think that is enough for now. We are neither of us in a mood for learning. I suggest we meet again tomorrow. What do you think, hm? At the same time?'

With a sigh Rosie sat down and unstrapped the skates, handing them back to the old man. 'I don't mean to get so angry,' she said. 'But, I don't know; it all seems so unfair sometimes.'

He smiled softly back at her, nodding. 'Tomorrow will be better. Then we will really begin to learn.'

She helped him with the wheelchair back towards the hotel before saying goodbye and heading for home. On the way she could not dismiss the image of the skate wheel spinning on and on without the slightest wobble to show its movement. It filled her with awe.

She drew level with Fore Street, still closed to traffic while workmen tore up the surface of the road. An open-backed lorry stood with its tailgate lowered. Two thick planks led up into it. Behind it a dumper truck waited to be driven up the planks into the back of the lorry. There were no workmen in sight.

But in their place Bernard and a few others, some of those who had been mocking Rosie and Mr Jackson, were hauling themselves into the back of the lorry and free-wheeling on their skates down the steep planks with squeals of delight.

Rosie would have gone the long way home, but they saw her before she had crossed the end of the road.

'There's Rosie. Got your new skates, Rosie? Come and have a go. We'll hold your hand.'

Rosie altered course, walking into Fore Street instead of straight on along the Esplanade. Her pride would not allow her to let them think she feared them; but she resolved, no matter what happened, to keep her temper.

Nothing did happen. When they saw her walking towards them the brave talk ceased. Instead they watched cautiously as she strolled past the lorry and round the corner. As soon as she was out of sight a nervous laugh went up.

Rosie could hear it, but she set her jaw and said nothing. Further down the street she came upon the workmen, examining a section of roadway.

She smiled grimly to herself. 'Excuse me.' The men looked up. 'There are some children round there playing on the back of your lorry.'

One of them eyed her narrowly, adjusted his belt and strode off to check. As she walked away she heard his voice, muffled by the corner, 'Gitorf, you ruddy tykes! Go on, out of it!'

Rosie continued home, satisfied, wondering what Mr Jackson would have said to that.

She heard her mother singing before she opened the front door. Lunch, she remembered, with Harry.

'Is that you, dear?'

'Yes; did you have a nice lunch?'

'Lovely, thank you.'

Her mother came out of the kitchen, into the hall. 'I thought I might invite him to tea one day; what do you think?'

Rosie smiled to herself. More surprises. Life was full of them.

'Up to you,' she said with a grin. 'I might not be able to make it. I'm in training.'

Six

The next few days were better than any Rosie could remember. Harry came for tea. It was obvious her mother liked him a lot, which was good because she sang more and smiled more.

And Harry had asked Rosie if she would help him stack the deckchairs for half an hour every evening after school. He was going to pay her.

It meant losing some skating time, but it would also bring her closer to the price of a new pair of roller-boots.

But even that did not matter so much anymore, thanks to Mr Jackson. And although she was pleased about Harry and her mum, and the extra money, and getting closer to her new boots, the best part was the time she spent with Mr Jackson and his magic skates.

She had been frightened of them at the beginning. After the first fall she was wary. They were as unpredict-able as a greased pole. Every time she rose to her feet they seemed to want to take off without her. The magic of the bearings seemed to separate her from reality. She felt as if she floated above the ground with eagle's wings at her ankles.

Little by little she grew used to them. Not as familiar as her old skates had felt, but it was coming. Her progress was good.

She clocked one minute six seconds; better than ever before! Mr Jackson showed her how to force extra effort from her legs, her arms, from her whole body in a controlled rhythmic flow that felt so good she couldn't help but laugh out loud with the joy of it as she arrowed her way, low and whispering, down the smooth strip of the Esplanade.

Mr Jackson was thrilled by the progress, too. He seemed to grow bigger in his wheelchair each time Rosie's speed improved.

When the Esplanade was too crowded for speed skating he would make Rosie find an empty spot in which to do exercises to improve her balance: jumps and spins and swallows, so that she seemed more ballet dancer than skater, and passers-by would stop and watch while Mr Jackson laughed and clapped, 'Bravo, miss. Bravo.'

Saturday came. She was up early with her mother, who had taken the day off from the supermarket to help Harry with the deckchairs.

'I've got some holiday due,' she said. 'And I'll be able to watch you skating. Harry says you're getting very good. I hope you keep out of Mr Scribbins' way now.'

Rosie snorted. 'He better keep out of my way – '

'Rosie! I won't have you talk like that. No matter what he's like.'

Rosie pulled a face, but her mother didn't see.

'Are you going to tear yourself away from Mr Jackson to have lunch with us?'

'Might,' said Rosie, poker-faced. 'Might go and annoy Scribbins instead.'

Her mother whirled round ready to explode, saw the smirk on Rosie's face and tugged affectionately at her hair instead.

They were about to open the front door when the newspaper dropped through the letterbox. Rosie had forgotten all about her meeting with Jim Kitchen. The smack of the newspaper onto the floor brought it all back

65

to her. She scooped it up and thumbed rapidly through it as she and her mother opened the door and walked down the garden path.

Rosie missed the page on her first search. They were well on their way when she finally found the piece Mr Kitchen had promised. She had been looking for something less prominent. She whooped with delight, punching at the air with her free hand.

The headline read, in big, black letters across the top of the page, 'Roller-skating Rosie leads the way!'

Slowing to a crawl her eyes popped and her grin spread wider as she read to her mother:

A 12-year-old girl with a passion for roller-skating has opened the route for a new annual event in Sidmouth's sporting calendar.

Rosie Swallow of Silver Street is determined to be the fastest person on eight wheels to cover the 491.38 metres from one end of the town's elegant Esplanade to the other.

With the help of the Sidmouth Gazette, in association with Sidmouth Round Table, she and the rest of the town's roller-skating rebels will get the chance to become Sidmouth Roller-Skater of the Year.

In two weeks Round Table members will start the first Sidmouth Roller-Skating Race from the yacht club flag-pole to the far end of the Esplanade.

Local charities will be invited to erect stalls along the Esplanade for the event. Permission has been sought to close the highway to traffic for the day.

The Sidmouth Gazette will present trophies to the winners, as well as cash prizes. Mr Hugh Norrish, chairman of Sidmouth Round Table, said, 'It's a great idea. It will draw the tourists into the town, and get the young people involved in a sport that is really catching on.

Some people have moaned about the roller-skating; but we believe it keeps the youngsters fit and healthy. Of course it needs controls, but what better way than this?

Rosie could hardly spit the words out, she was so excited. She was gripping her mother's elbow hard as she hurried through the report. When she reached the end she leapt in the air and yelled, 'Yahoo!' Privately she warmed herself on the best bit – Scribbins would be purple with fury.

She hopped and jumped and squirmed on her mother's arm. 'A race,' she breathed. 'I'm going to win a race.' It never occurred to Rosie that she might not win. The picture in her mind was as vivid and solid as television.

Dreams appeared in pastel colours and shapes that didn't fit into reality. Their pictures were blurred at the edges. But this was a different picture; this was painted in colours clean as air, detailed down to the expressions on the faces of the cheering crowd.

They were cheering Rosie as she streamed past them in a blur, over the asphalt, across the winning line into the laughing arms of Harry and Mr Jackson and her mum. And Bernard would come second, but no-one would notice him as the crowd milled around Rosie. 'Well done, Rosie . . . Brilliant . . . best ever.'

And the time . . . Rosie would shrug off the congratulations, cutting her way through the throng to reach the time-keeper. And on his table would be the official clock: big as a plate, with only a second hand to mark the passing of that one, brief, vital minute. As the crowd parted she would see it: the hand nearly vertical, the tip of it stopped at . . . it wouldn't matter as long as it was under a minute.

67

The crowd's cheers would rise to another crescendo as the announcement was made over the loudspeaker system that Rosie Swallow had achieved the one-minute dream!

'Who said you're going to win?' asked a voice.

'Uh?' The picture in her thoughts collapsed like a spilled jigsaw as she absorbed her mother's question. ''Course I'll win. I've got Mr Jackson's skates and I'm doing better and better times. And I haven't even got used to them yet. I'll win; and I'll do it in less than a minute.'

Her mother smiled. She would have been angry if it had sounded like boasting, but it hadn't. Rosie made her claim in the firm conviction that there was no other alternative. It was unthinkable in Rosie's mind that the result could be any different.

'If she wants it hard enough,' her mother thought, 'she'll probably get it.'

At the beach Rosie left her mother's side and raced on foot – she had left her skates at home because she had taken to using Mr Jackson's all the time – to where Harry was erecting a long line of deckchairs that billowed in the wind.

She showed him the story, bouncing from one foot to the other as he read.

He grinned hugely. 'Two weeks. That's not long. Can you do it?'

'Do what?'

'Get your time down to sixty seconds.'

She nodded smugly.

Harry's face clouded. 'I know someone who's not going to like it – Scribbins.'

'Ha! He won't dare come near,' Rosie answered. 'All talk.'

'Well, don't get too cocky, Wonder-Woman. It won't

be like skating on your own. Races are different; harder. What if you don't win?'

'I won't if I stand round talking to you all day,' she grinned. She raced down the Esplanade to where she could see Mr Jackson looking at his watch under the flagpole.

Before he could comment on her lateness she thrust the newspaper into his hand. He saw immediately how keenly excited she was. He read quietly while she danced on the spot beside him.

'Hmmm.'

'Have you finished?' she asked eagerly.

He nodded.

'Well?'

'Hmmm.'

Rosie's jiggling slowed to a stop. She put her hands on her hips. 'Is that all?'

He looked up at her. She was surprised to see a sadness on his face. The twinkle in his eyes had faded and the wrinkles at the corners gathered themselves into a pained expression.

Rosie was bewildered. 'What's the matter?'

He paused; then with a long, deep sigh he said quickly, as if he had made up his mind about something, 'I don't like races.'

'What's the difference. If I'm fastest – I'm fastest. Does it matter if it's in a race or not?'

He gripped her hand in one of his, rough and boney. He had never done that before. It was cold.

'Rosie,' he said softly, 'When I watched you skating here every morning, so early in the morning, so dedicated, what I liked was that you weren't concerned about beating anybody.

'You just wanted to do the best that you could do. Just

you. You set a target: one minute to get from here to there.' He indicated the far end of the Esplanade. 'Your own target. You said you would be happy once you had done it. You didn't want to beat anyone. Why beat anyone? What does that prove, hm?'

'How do I know I'm the best if I don't beat the others?' wailed Rosie impatiently.

'You'll never beat the others,' he answered simply.

Rosie opened her mouth in indignation, but he cut her short. 'You might beat the ones who come here for this race. You probably will. But there are other people in the world who are better than you. Faster.

'And if they aren't now they will be one day. You can't be best. No-one ever is. You can set a record for now; but one day someone will beat it.' He looked at her sternly. 'But – if you are as good as you possibly can be; if you set yourself a test, and pass it . . . that's very special.'

She drew her hand away, sulkily. 'Does that mean you won't help me?'

The steely bright light came back into his eyes as he wagged a finger at Rosie. 'Do not talk to me like that, miss. Hm? I will continue to believe that your real aim is personal endeavour, and I will help. You have a lot to learn. The world does not revolve around you and you are not necessarily the most important person in it. However, you have spirit. And a disarming smile.' His eyes twinkled. 'I will help you, Rosie Swallow, but watch your manners, hm?'

Rosie flushed, and a bright grin flashed across her face. She sat down. As the old man unwrapped the skates from the bundle on his lap he said, 'If this race is only two weeks away we must manage as much practice as possible this week. Next week may not be so easy because I have

70

found somewhere to live and it may be more difficult to get down to the Esplanade whenever I wish.'

'I could come and push you,' said Rosie, strapping on the skates. 'What's it called?'

'The Valley Residential Home for the Elderly.' He smiled. 'I certainly qualify, hm? Most of them look like fossils. But the couple who run it seem most charming. Very eager to help. I'm sure they will run me down to the Esplanade. They have a vehicle especially designed to take wheelchairs. And if you really would come and wheel me out sometimes I'm sure I shall keep very busy.

'I shall be very sorry,' he added wistfully, 'when this race is over.'

'Why? I thought you didn't approve.'

'Nor I do. But once you've done it our time together will be over.'

Rosie was aghast. She had somehow thought of her time with this very proper old man going on forever. Until that moment she had thought that she went along only for the skates and the training; but the idea that it would all come to an end saddened her. She had grown quite fond of him.

'I can still take you out,' she said. 'I can wheel you around. It'd have to be round here, though,' she added thoughtfully. Then with a grin, 'We'd never get you on the bus.'

He smiled. 'That's a kind thought, Rosie. Kind thought. If the vehicle at the home has room for a wheelchair, I'm sure they could squeeze in a little thing like you, too – We'll have to ask Mr and Mrs Scribbins.'

Rosie was cheerfully strapping the second skate to her foot. It took two seconds for his words to sink in. One. Two. No more than that. The name surged into her ears

71

in an acid stream, punching into her stomach in a frozen wall of ice. Her heart pumped and her chest hurt.

She looked up and for one brief, rocky moment Mr Jackson appeared to recede like a face rushing away down a tunnel. The light faded around her and she put out a hand to steady herself, and all the time she heard the words, etching themselves into her brain like a nail scratching on slate, 'We'll have to ask Scribbins . . . Scribbins . . . Scribbins . . .'

'Rosie . . .? Rosie, are you all right?'

Her head cleared, and quickly her eyes focussed on the worried face of Mr Jackson, studying her, puzzled: 'What on earth's the matter, hm?'

'Scr-Scribbins,' she stuttered. 'Is that their name?'

'The nursing home? Yes.'

'You can't . . .' she began.

'Rosie, what on earth are you saying, hm?'

Rosie shivered. The day was bright. It was sunny and warm; yet Rosie felt as if all the clouds of the world were heaped in a dark, ominous bank over her head.

'They're awful,' she stumbled. 'Awful. They don't like anyone. Horrible. They'll hurt you. You mustn't go.'

The old man's moustache bristled, and he said firmly, 'Nonsense, miss. I have met them several times. Talked to the residents. Wonderful place. I shall enjoy myself. And I'm sure you will, too. Now stop behaving like an actress.'

Rosie flushed and winced at his words. 'That's what they pretend,' she said. 'But ask anyone. Honestly. Ask Harry. They shut the old people up and poison them.'

'Rosie!' Mr Jackson's normally rigid, thin mouth fell open in horror.

'You've only got to see them,' she blundered on. 'They look like they're going to die any minute. The Scribbinses

72

do that to them. They don't like anyone. It was them that tried to knock me off the Esplanade; they just rammed into me –'

Mr Jackson's open hand slammed down on to the arm of the wheelchair. 'That-will-do!' he shouted, emphasizing each word in his strong, clear voice. 'After all the slander we finally get the truth, hm?' he stormed. 'The Scribbinses have got in your way, and that doesn't suit Miss Rosie Swallow. I will not hear these things!'

Rosie's bottom lip began to wobble. His fierceness frightened her, but it wasn't fair. She could cry or she could get angry, or maybe both together. The feeling of injustice that had struck her so many times before, came flooding back.

'How do you know?' she shouted back. 'Anyone can see they're awful just by looking. Like vultures!'

'Rosie!'

'Least, anyone with any sense can see!' With that last, final insult she buried her head in her hands and wept.

The old man watched her grimly for a few moments. His moustache moved up and down as his mouth worked in the struggle to calm himself.

'So; you throw stones at me now, hm? Well, I will tell you, miss. I am more than eighty years old. It is quite possible that I have met in my lifetime more people than you have even seen in yours.

'I have some experience in the judgement of character. I believe I have been wrong in my judgement only two or three times in my life.

'Now, let us take this present situation. It is unlikely that your opinion is correct because you do not have any experience. That is the best we can hope.

'At worst you are a spoiled little girl who wants her

own way too much. I hope not; for that would show my judgement to be wrong in one more case – yours!

'If you are the girl I think you are then you will regret what you have said and you will apologize for it. I do not expect you to do so now, but I shall be here again tomorrow.' He looked at his watch. 'At this time.

'If we are to continue I shall expect to find you here prepared to express some element of contrition. If you are not here then I shall admit a misjudgement of character.'

His hands moved to swing the wheelchair round; but the small, crushed figure of Rosie burst fiercely into action.

She tore off first one skate, then the other, sobbing angrily as she did so. 'P'raps you're right,' she seethed. 'P'raps your judgement's wrong about me – and about them, too.

'It's only 'cos I like you. And all you can do is act like some stuffy old teacher or something.' She flung down the skates. 'Well, who cares. Who cares!'

She dashed one arm savagely across her tear-stained face and runny nose, turned on her heel and fled.

Mr Jackson watched her go, sadly shaking his head. With difficulty he reached the skates on the asphalt where Rosie had thrown them, wrapped them again in their old green cloth and, turning the wheelchair round, headed back to his hotel.

Seven

Rosie went straight home. Confused, frustrated and hurt, she threw herself down on her bed and wept. Her feelings were so many and varied that she could barely endure thinking at all; but she couldn't empty her mind of them, either.

There was Mr Jackson: he was a funny, stiff old thing, but she had grown to like him a lot. He was stern, but he had been fair with her. Like when Bernard and the others had laughed. And he had been loyal, too, despite his gruffness.

There was the race: she knew she could win it. Even in her old skates she would win it. She had two weeks for practice, and if she wasn't going to use Mr Jackson's skates she would have to practise every spare minute of the day with her old ones – into the night if necessary; if her mother would let her.

And then, of course, there were the others. Those, like Bernard, who would also have read the Sidmouth Gazette. Maybe people from other towns would get to hear about the race. Mr Jackson was right; there would be others, older than her, maybe, with better skates, who would seek to win the prizes.

Maybe she could do more work for Harry and get together enough money to buy new skates in time for the race. But if she did that she would have no time left to grow familiar with them.

And over everything seemed to hang the shadow of the

Scribbinses. They seemed to be lurking somewhere in all the corners of her life, waiting for the moment to spoil everything.

They had picked the right moment this time, she reflected grimly. Without being anywhere near they had managed to get back at her – just as they had promised – and they probably didn't even know it.

Now Mr Jackson, poor Mr Jackson, was going to live with them. She couldn't bear it. She wanted to shake him until he saw things her way. He couldn't have looked closely at their eyes or he would know instinctively that the Scribbinses were cruel.

But if he was so clever! If he knew so much better, then let him find out for himself! Why should she care! But she *did* care. She remembered those sad, grey figures in their wheelchairs the day she first met the Scribbinses, and her skin prickled as she thought of Mr Jackson, who was so bright and alive and enthusiastic, growing to be like them.

The more she thought, the more she knew she would have to go back the next day and apologize. Maybe he would find out before it was too late. Maybe she could find some more subtle way of showing him she was right.

And in any case, it was really too late to abandon him. There were only two weeks before the race. Two weeks in which to be sure she could achieve what had never been achieved before: skating the Esplanade in less than a minute.

The next morning she went back to the Esplanade to seek out Mr Jackson. Her stomach churned as she approached it, but when she reached the flagpole no-one was there. She waited, sitting on the edge of the seawall, her legs dangling over the beach below.

She heard the clearing of a throat behind her. Mr Jackson was sitting by the flagpole in his wheelchair; a

76

man from the hotel was walking away. Rosie noticed immediately that the bundle containing the skates was on Mr Jackson's lap.

He smiled at her, and in his eyes she saw the twinkling blue light that always made her smile. And smile she did, but softly, with her head hung.

He spoke first. 'I'm glad you came. I thought you might not.'

'I wasn't going to at first, but ... I'm sorry, Mr Jackson,' she blurted, tears welling up in her eyes again. 'I never –'

He took hold of her hand.

'I know,' he said. 'There is nothing more to say. We are still friends, aren't we, hm? Right. Get these skates on. We lost all yesterday, and time is something we can no longer afford.'

He held the bundle out to her. Instead of taking it she swept his hand aside and threw her arms round his neck, squeezing hard.

He laughed. It was a long, ringing, happy laugh, and when she looked up his bright eyes had a film of wet over them.

'Well, well; if you break a leg it will still have been worth it for that,' he said, grinning.

The day went well. Somehow the intensity of the previous day's emotions had swept away a little of the formality between them. Rosie felt Mr Jackson was kinder in some way she couldn't describe. She tried hard to follow his advice; to impress him with her progress. And she found that now the excitement of the newspaper report had cleared away she didn't really care much about beating anyone else. Foremost in her thoughts was not winning the race, but breaking the one-minute barrier.

She got little chance that day to discover whether she

had progressed. After a couple of warming-up passes along the Esplanade the warm weather began to bring the people out. She and Mr Jackson were obliged to give up the long distance.

Instead he made her practice exercises to strengthen her legs and improve her balance.

In the afternoon Bernard and two friends appeared on the Esplanade, intent on practice. To her surprise Rosie found she didn't mind their presence. They stood and watched her for a while as Mr Jackson gave her instructions and she carried them out; and what he urged her to do, they did also. Rosie and Bernard caught each other's eye and a trace of a smile crossed both faces before they were once again intent on their practice.

When finally Mr Jackson announced that he was returning to the hotel to rest, they all pushed him there, and then walked home together, stopping at the Fore Street roadworks to skate down the planks. This time Rosie kept a lookout. She had felt mean about sneaking on them since she had done it. She told herself this would make amends.

The next five days were school days. Rosie was ready and skating by 7.30 every morning. But for Mr Jackson that was too early. It took him a great deal of time to dress himself and then there was breakfast, and he felt the early morning cold. But he would watch from the window, waving to let her know he was there.

In the evenings, after school, he met her and made comments on what he had observed.

Only once during the week did she try again to raise the subject of the Scribbinses, but Mr Jackson would not hear her. Some of the old fierceness returned as he held up his hand and said, 'Rosie! Don't spoil it.' After that she kept off the subject, recognizing that there was no hope of persuading him to think again. Indeed, she feared the Scribbinses might be blackening her name, for he was bound to be in touch with them if he was moving within a week. Better to keep away from the subject.

Before the week was over she had cut back her best time to one minute five seconds.

Only five seconds! She marvelled at the way in which such a little space of time could seem so long when the Esplanade railings were in sight. It was an agonizing period: five brief ticks of a clock that she seemed unable to bridge; and as the week came to an end she became more irritated with herself.

Mr Jackson noticed. 'If you lose your temper you will destroy your chances,' he warned. 'You can do it, we both know it, but you must be calm. You must be free to concentrate on every stride you make.'

'But you'll be gone after the weekend,' she wailed. 'We won't have any time.'

He smiled. 'Young lady, two things: firstly, you are the skater. I am delighted that you feel you need me still, but in the end I must say – only you can do it.

'Secondly: we will continue to see plenty of each other. As you said, you can if you wish bring me down here yourself. I would be delighted if you did. It will mean forgetting this nonsense about Mr and Mrs Scribbins and The Valley Residential Home, but that is up to you. I will be observing to see how you manage the dilemma.'

She sensed he was laughing at her, but it didn't seem like a cruel laugh. She snorted. 'I'm not scared of them.'

'Nor have you any reason to be.' He waved the subject away.

'Now, tomorrow is Saturday. We shall have all day. I am afraid Sunday is the day I move and I will be busy organizing my belongings and a few pieces of furniture which will take most of my time. So let us make a full day of tomorrow.'

He smiled. 'I have a feeling it will be the day you finally break through.'

She grinned back at him. 'Now or never, I suppose.'

She wheeled him back to the hotel, sharing a companionable silence until they reached the steps to the entrance, where one of the staff came and took over. He waved goodbye fondly and she waved back, then turned for home.

Next day Rosie was up early, joining her mother in the kitchen.

'I'm going to do it today.'

Rosie struggled into a pair of shorts.

'Do what, dear? Isn't it cold for shorts.'

'Mr Jackson says it will help cut down wind resistance. I'm going to do the Esplanade. In under a minute. You going to come and watch?'

'You'll have to do it at lunchtime, then. I'm working, don't forget.'

Rosie was putting on her trainers. She looked up. 'Tell you what: I'll do it this morning and when you come down I'll do it again for you and Harry.'

'Big head!' Her mother stopped washing the breakfast dishes and turned to face Rosie. She looked down at her daughter. 'Rosie,' she said gently, 'You mustn't mind if it doesn't happen.'

'Mind!' shrieked Rosie in mock horror. 'I'll kill myself!'

'Rosie! Don't say that! Not even in fun. When you get an idea in your head you get so . . . blinkered. There are lots more things in the world besides skating, you know.'

Rosie's good humour could not be quelled. 'No problem,' she said. 'We'll do the one minute today. Next

Saturday we'll win the race, and then we'll find something else to do. You can choose.'

'How about a holiday? Harry's invited us.'

Rosie stopped halfway to the door. She spun round, eyes wide with delight. 'No!' she gasped, overwhelmed.

'Yes.'

'When?'

'End of next month. He's going to get someone in to handle the deckchairs.'

'Where?'

'We thought Greece might be nice . . .'

Rosie leapt in the air with a shout. She shot into her mother's arms and squeezed. 'I knew today was going to be special.'

She planted a kiss on her mother's lowered cheek and headed, skipping, for the door. She paused there and with a grin asked, 'Can I take my skates?'

Her mother reached for the dishcloth and hurled it at Rosie, but she was gone.

Rosie bounced. She bounced and she grinned and the people who passed her on the street were first puzzled and then infected; and they went on their way feeling a little better than they had before.

She went the short way through Fore Street and ran up the planks that still sloped out from the back of the lorry, heedless of the workmen who were all around preparing for the day's work.

'Oi!' shouted one. Rosie laughed and leapt over the side of the lorry, waving goodbye as she did so, leaving the workmen scratching their heads.

The deckchairs were out along the Esplanade and she bounced and skipped down the line of them until she met Harry, unfolding yet another. She bounced up to him and with an extra skip she found the height to plant a kiss on his cheek.

'Well, well!' he laughed. 'Free deckchairs all day for you.'

'You deserved it,' she said demurely.

'For what?'

'Mum told me about the holiday.'

'My pleasure,' specially if I get another kiss.' He bent down and Rosie gave him one.

'I'm going to do it today,' she grinned.

'Do what?'

She tutted in exasperation. 'That's what Mum said. The Esplanade. In one minute. Going to watch?'

'I wouldn't miss it for anything.'

She bounced off down the asphalt, looking around her. Everything was working out fine. The weather was a little too cool to encourage many people out early. The Esplanade was empty, which would give her a clear run. She felt fit and keen and indomitable.

She saw Mr Jackson under the flagpole at the end of the Esplanade. She was in mid-wave when the bright, soaring bubble of her thoughts burst and vanished.

Behind the wheelchair, grim as pall-bearers, were Mr and Mrs Scribbins. The wind scoured at Rosie's legs and she shivered. Her steps faltered in mid-stride, the bounce vanished, and her feet felt as if they were dragging through glue. The sun receded until its thin, yellow glint served only to accentuate the frost that gripped her.

Mr Jackson was beckoning her forward. She wanted to turn and run. She raised her hands to her ears imagining, hopelessly, that she could block everything out.

Mr Jackson was beckoning still, more urgently. There was the vaguest smudge of a smile on Mrs Scribbins' face. Her chin was up and her head was topped by a shapeless black hat with feathers that stuck out spikily like her hair. She looked triumphantly down her hooked, hawk's nose.

Rosie flushed. For the briefest moment she felt her spirit leave her. All the light and brightness drained out of her as efficiently as if a plug had been pulled. She felt limp as a rag.

But as she stood, looking into the cold eyes of Mrs Scribbins, the hole in Rosie filled with resentment.

She set her mouth in a thin, firm line and stepped forward. It wasn't fair that these . . . people, should step into her life and destroy it. Her eyes flicked from Mr Jackson to the couple behind him; first the man, then the woman. 'You can't stop me,' she thought. 'This is my day. You won't stop me.'

They looked back at her. The triumph was still emblazoned across their faces, lending to them the faintest trace of a smile; giving nothing away but a subtle shout of triumph.

Rosie dismissed them from her gaze and smiled warmly at Mr Jackson.

He said: 'Good morning, miss. Good morning. I'd like you to say hello to Mr and Mrs Scribbins. I've told them all about you and your offer to bring me down here sometimes. As I move in tomorrow I thought it a good idea that you should meet them now. They were very keen to meet you, too.'

Rosie glanced up at them without expression, and looked back to Mr Jackson. 'I wish you'd told me first.'

'Rosie,' he murmured sharply. 'Show some respect. Say hello.'

Before she could respond a shadow fell on her and the face of Mrs Scribbins peered down, close to hers. The feathers jiggled crazily in her hat as she spoke. 'She's probably shy. You mustn't scold.'

Her breath smelled sickly sweet and her teeth were big and tainted with brown stains. Rosie turned her head away. Mrs Scribbins reached out with both hands. One took Rosie's resistant arm while the other took her hand and shook it firmly.

'So this is the little girl who has been wearing poor Mr Jackson out so much. We're so pleased to meet you; Rosie, is it?'

Rosie wrenched her arm free. She was aware of the grim face of Mr Jackson looking steadily back at her. From where he sat he could not see that the soulless smile on Mrs Scribbins' face had turned to a malicious grin.

His jaw hardened and a deadly fury set in his eyes. Silently he unwound the skates from their bundle and handed them to her. She sat and strapped them on, head bowed, while the Scribbinses prattled: 'I do think skating is so healthy for young people,' said Mr Scribbins. 'Of course, it has always been a source of sadness to Mrs Scribbins and myself that we never had children. A terrible burden . . .'

Rosie growled inwardly, finished strapping the skates, and stood up. Mr Jackson waved her away. 'Warm up,' he ordered brusquely.

Rosie turned away, dispirited. She cruised along the empty Esplanade, doing automatically the exercises he had taught her. It all seemed heavy and hopeless. She returned reluctantly to Mr Jackson. The Scribbinses were still behind him, still triumphant.

Mr Jackson looked smaller, sadder. Rosie could see she had disappointed him. She longed to make some gesture that would cure his mood, help him cure hers. But with the thin, dark figures of the Scribbinses behind him there was nothing she could do.

He looked dully at her, and breathed a deep and final

sigh. 'Well, see what you can do, anyway,' he murmured. 'Once up the Esplanade and back again. Is it worth me timing you?'

Rosie looked at the ground. 'Not if you don't want to.'

He wasn't even looking at her. 'Go on then.'

As Rosie turned to go Mr Scribbins interrupted. 'You'll pardon us if we leave you for a minute or two, Mr Jackson? We have left Millie further down the Esplanade with some of the others. We had better make sure she hasn't wheeled them into the sea.' He passed Mr Jackson a conspiratorial grin over the joke.

As they loped silently away Rosie turned to Mr Jackson quickly, as though the chance might be gone very soon. 'I'm sorry,' she pleaded. 'Really I am. Please, Mr Jackson . . .'

He smiled, still not looking at her. Some of the hardness had gone out of his face, but it was clear he felt hurt. 'Never mind, hm? I suppose we can't all get on with everyone. But – ' he stiffened once more, 'that is no excuse for bad manners.'

'Mr Jackson?'

'Hm?'

'Please don't go.'

He looked at her at last and he sounded tired. 'Enough of that. It is all fixed. I suppose . . . I suppose I won't be seeing much of you after all?'

Rosie could feel the tears rising. She looked down, not answering.

'Go on,' he said. 'Up the Esplanade. I'm timing you. Try not to waste this last day.'

But she did waste it. There was no effort left in her. She reached the railings at the far end and, without waiting to see if Mr Jackson's hand was raised to start her again, she headed back to him. She was merely cruising, she knew, wondering all the time whether it would be better to give up the whole thing: the race, the dream, Mr Jackson.

She was still contemplating this when she drew level with the Scribbinses. She would not have noticed, but for a murmured whimper from Millie as she passed. She looked up and saw Millie staring wide-eyed at the ground in front of Rosie.

Rosie followed her gaze and saw, in the one atom of time before she sped into them, a blanket of scattered pebbles strewn across her path.

Had Rosie been really trying as she should have been then Millie's cry would not have saved her. The small pebbles would have locked her wheels instantly and Rosie's hurtling body would have crashed to the asphalt at appalling speed. But Rosie had just enough time to see the danger and take action.

One skate had already stopped abruptly on the pebbles. The other foot came crashing down amid the stones and she keeled and stumbled through, spinning and tripping in an effort to stay on her feet. The incredible bearings on Mr Jackson's skates did their job too well, and just as Rosie thought she was clear and safe, the wheels spun out from under her.

The street scene vanished as her head flicked back. The wide, blue sky was all she could see as she gritted her teeth for the sickening crack as her back and head hit the ground.

It never came. A pair of strong arms held her; and where the sun and sky had been Harry's face appeared upside down, smiling with relief. 'Didn't think I was going to make it,' he said. 'I reckon you owe me another kiss for that. Didn't your mum tell you to be careful?'

He straightened her up, scraping the pebbles aside with

the edge of his shoe. He hadn't seen the Scribbinses, and Rosie didn't point them out to him. She turned to him, a grim smile on her face. 'Thank you,' she said. 'I was being careful.'

She was gone before Harry could reply.

Eight

'Sorry,' she said to Mr Jackson on her return. 'Fell over.' She said nothing about the Scribbinses nor the pebbles.

Mr Jackson raised his eyebrows. 'Unlike you nowadays, hm? Concentrate, miss. Concentrate.'

'I haven't warmed up properly. Can we do some more exercises?'

Mr Jackson sensed a change of attitude. 'That's the spirit,' he said cheerfully. 'Off you go.'

For a while she stayed near him, putting herself through a series of rigorous exercises, planning her next step. It was clear the Scribbinses could not stay all day on the Esplanade with their wheelchair charges. She decided she would wait them out. She would remain alert, and she would give back some of what she had taken.

Her eyes fixed upon the Scribbinses far off along the Esplanade. She set off down the footpath at cruising speed. One glance behind told her that Mr Jackson was gazing out to sea. Quickly she vaulted the low wall between the path and the road, and crossed the road to the other pavement where she was partially hidden by the parked cars.

She sped off, parallel with the Esplanade, but on the far side of the road from it, until she was a little way behind the Scribbinses.

Quickly she crossed the road again, back to the Esplanade, and with all her skill she pushed her speed to the maximum, closing fast and silently on the Scribbinses and their wheelchairs. Mrs Scribbins was the only one without a wheelchair to push. She was walking against the low dividing wall. Beside her was Mr Scribbins and Millie was nearest the sea.

Rosie knew what to do. It was something she had never tried before, but that would add to the surprise. As the distance between them closed rapidly she crouched low. When she seemed so close that she must cannon into Mrs Scribbins' back she leapt deftly onto the low wall, agile as a cat.

She screamed past Mrs Scribbins. Rosie's arm flicked out and knocked the black hat forward over the woman's eyes.

The tall figure went rigid with shock. As Rosie whizzed by Mrs Scribbins gave a shriek of horror that was cut off in mid-breath and Rosie turned to see her being lowered, trembling, onto the wall by Mr Scribbins.

Rosie continued along the Esplanade, a wicked grin on her face. No-one had seen, for there were few people on the Esplanade and none in the vicinity. And who would believe that anyone could have skated by at such a speed on such a narrow surface?

She crossed once more to the far side of the road and sped back to Mr Jackson; but not before Mr Scribbins had spotted her. He shook his fist and his lip curled as he stormed a string of silent invective. She ignored it. On her way she bought an ice-cream at the roadside kiosk.

'I lost sight of you,' said Mr Jackson when she reached him.

She held up the ice-cream. 'Hungry,' she replied. She looked down the Esplanade. Mr Scribbins was hurrying towards them, leaving his wife and Millie far behind, slowly pushing the wheelchairs.

When he reached them his face was mask-white. The

only sign of his rage was a maze of red veins that patterned his face. Rosie braced herself for the storm, but instead Mr Scribbins merely smiled a hard smile and said, 'Do forgive us for leaving you for so long Mr Jackson. We like to ensure that everyone gets a good long walk along the Esplanade.'

'He's not going to say anything,' thought Rosie. 'It's war!'

She waited warily for his next move. It came quickly.

'Has Rosie done it yet?' he asked brightly, glancing from her to Mr Jackson.

The old man looked at Rosie. 'I told him about the one-minute business.' Then to Mr Scribbins he said, 'Not yet. I don't think she's up to it today.'

'Oh, what a pity. Couldn't she have just one try. I know our other residents . . .' He indicated the wheelchairs along the Esplanade, where they had stopped, '. . . would love to see her try. We've told them all about it. But I suppose if she's not good enough,' he sighed.

Rosie sneered. Not good enough! Her eyes narrowed. Carefully she studied the Esplanade. She felt contempt for Scribbins if he thought she would be caught a second time by a wheelchair thrust across her path. This time there would be too many people watching. She would warn Harry and her mother before she started; and there would be Mr Jackson, too, all looking out for trouble. And just in case, she would keep well over to the beach edge to give her the greatest chance to anticipate any tricks.

She smiled sweetly up at Mr Scribbins. 'I'd love to try for you,' she crooned.

Mr Jackson's mouth dropped open in surprise, but he did not see the reaction on Mr Scribbins' face as Rosie blinked innocently up at him. Scribbins scowled and said nothing.

'But I promised my mum I'd wait until she was watching. I'll just go and see if she's here yet.'

She skated to the deckchairs and Harry while Mr Scribbins joined his wife. Rosie arrived as her mother did.

'Done it yet?' asked her mother.

'Been waiting for you. Better watch carefully. You only get one chance.'

Harry beamed. He put his arm round her mother's shoulder. 'We've both got our fingers crossed. Good luck.'

'By the way,' added Rosie. 'The Scribbinses are here. Keep your eyes open for me.'

Harry winked in understanding. 'Promise,' he said.

With a last grim smile and a wave Rosie was gone. She rejoined Mr Jackson, her stomach boiling with anticipation.

Mr Jackson was concerned. 'Are you sure you are ready for this, Rosie. Hm? Remember: patience is the secret. If you let anything rattle you, you'll never do it.'

Rosie took a deep breath. She nodded. 'I'm ready. Let's do it. And Mr Jackson – thank you for everything.'

Mr Jackson smiled, squeezed her hand and let it go. 'Prepare yourself in your own time. Remember the breathing.'

Rosie put her hands to the back of her neck and stretched her elbow outwards until her shoulder blades touched. She exhaled and felt the tension float out on her breath. A laugh broke free, taking her by surprise.

It was a perfect day. Cool, grey, but with no threat of rain. Before her stretched an empty Esplanade. Empty except for a few scattered pedestrians, her mother and

Harry sitting on the beach steps – and the Scribbinses, hunched over the low dividing wall.

Despite the chill they cast on her Rosie knew she was going to do it. She could see it as clearly as if it was a picture in a frame. Her body felt right, keen to be started. Her mind had an iron dedication. So many good reasons: for Mr Jackson, her mother and Harry; for herself, especially for herself.

And for the Scribbinses. The sweet, sugar topping on the cake would be their faces when the cheer went up for Rosie.

She positioned herself beside the flagpole, leaning into the path ahead, poised and ready. She shook the excitement down through her wrists and out of her hands, breathed slowly out and without looking round, nodded to Mr Jackson. 'OK,' she said.

Mr Jackson quietly commentated, 'I'm waiting for the full minute to come round . . . fifteen seconds . . . ten . . . five . . . Marks, set, go!'

His voice was already faint and distant before the final word had died away.

Rosie was a blur. Her first stride seemed to cover metres; as if there were some force behind her, pushing. Her second was a graceful sweep and by the third her body, curved over and only centimetres from the ground, was already parting the air with a ripping hiss. And she knew, in that first ten seconds, that the victory would be hers. She felt as if she could take her feet from the ground and fly. The rushing air made it hard to breath but still she found more reserves, more power.

She favoured the beach side, aware now that she drew nearer the Scribbinses. She streamed up to them; level with them; sucking up from the well of her willpower an increase in rhythm, in power, in speed. Then she knew – sure as a hammer falling – that she had lost.

It was only a movement in the corner of her vision. A mere flick but Rosie knew, as surely as she felt her spirit drowning inside her, that it was over.

The movement was a walking stick that had been laid at Mr Scribbins' feet. One sharp, furtive kick had sent it snaking out from beside a wheelchair, sliding across the asphalt. She was helpless as it slithered to a stop inside her stride. Her right foot was already travelling down on to it, unstoppable, doomed. She felt her skate scoop up the stick, the cane handle whipping forward, cracking viciously against her left calf. As she flung out her hands in front of her all that she saw was the surge of the asphalt into her face. Even with her hands out to protect her she felt the searing pain as her cheek bounced off the ground and skidded forward.

The breath was rammed out of her body by the force of the impact and tiny grains of grit and beach sand ground through the palms of her hands. But none of it was pain compared with the agony in her knee. Though she didn't hear it, a clear, fine scream strained out of her throat as her knees speared into the asphalt. Her body twisted to one side as she fell, and one knee rose. The other ploughed the asphalt, grating away first the skin, then the flesh to a raw, red pulp. Her scream died away, as she came to a stop, leaving one skate clear of the ground with the wheels spinning aimlessly, noiselessly.

A fog clouded Rosie's brain. She would have slid into oblivion, but for the pain in her knee. It clawed her mind back to consciousness.

She heard many footsteps, and urgent voices. She looked up and saw only the blur of legs approaching. The pain in her knee rushed away and speared back again,

93

forcing her eyes into focus. There were long legs in front of her. A man's. She could hear other steps, but as she dragged herself up on an elbow and looked higher, her eyes met those in the gaunt face of Mr Scribbins.

There was a humourless, satisfied glint in his eyes. His mouth was drawn tight, corners tracing an upward curve, and the whole sum of his expression was victory. And his victory was sweeter for he saw in Rosie the certain knowledge that she, too, knew she was beaten.

Tears came then, not from pain, but from anger at herself. An anger that flashed and bubbled and spat inside her until it burst through all feeling: through pain, humiliation, disappointment; until it burst out of her like a fountain of molten rock.

She grabbed hold of the railings and dragged herself up. As she did so her free hand closed on a stone, a large round pebble from the beach, big as her fist, that had been discarded there. She stood, and her lip curled as she rose, and drew her arm back.

Mr Scribbins had stopped a few yards off, still triumphant, still smirking.

'I hate you,' she screamed; and her arm flung out.

She heard a voice; Harry's voice, 'Rosie, no!'

But it came too late. She had let go of the stone. It travelled as though through water, seeming to take minutes to pass the few feet between her and Mr Scribbins.

She saw his eyes fix on it, and in that moment when it should have struck him, he stepped aside.

With mounting horror she watched the stone curve and drop towards the wheelchairs and the head of a frail old man sitting in one of them.

There was only one sound: a brief, dull smack, and the stone spun away. The head fell forward, and a thread of blood ran from the wound, over the scalp, and dripped onto the knobs of the grey knuckles where they twitched involuntarily on the lap.

Rosie was paralysed with horror, all pain forgotten. A voice inside her prayed, 'Give me that moment again. Oh please, someone, give me that moment again.'

A stricken cry made her turn. They were all there, they had all seen it: Mr Jackson, who had come up quickly in his wheelchair; her mother; Harry; the Scribbinses. Even Millie was staring at her aghast, gnawing her knuckle.

She looked from face to face, but none of them knew her. Each one showed horror, a fear almost.

Rosie was bewildered. She searched for eyes that were open to her and found none. Her heart began to pound. 'I . . . I didn't mean to . . .' she blurted.

Mr Scribbins had retreated back to the still figure of the old man in the wheelchair. His eyes narrowed cunningly. 'He dropped his walking stick,' he whined. 'Poor old chap. Couldn't help it.' And then, looking up accusingly at Rosie, 'How could she?'

Rosie gasped. The hair on the back of her neck prickled and her spine froze. Ice crystals formed in her stomach.

'No!' she cried. 'No. I wouldn't! He kicked it. Scribbins kicked it out at me. It was deliberate!'

With a drowning feeling the truth came to Rosie. 'You didn't see him!' she uttered, aghast. 'You didn't see him.' She covered her face with her arms and sobbed into the railings.

The spell was broken. It had seemed to take minutes, but took only seconds. Harry was the first to move. He thrust Rosie's mother towards the weeping girl. 'Take her home,' he ordered. '*Now*. And stay with her. I'll get an ambulance.'

As he ran to find a phone Scribbins called out, 'And the police. Get the police, too.'

95

Mrs Scribbins, still inscrutable, face still a desert of emotion, folded a handkerchief into a pad and held it disdainfully to the old man's head wound.

Rosie's mother gently prised the sobbing body away from the railings and led it away.

A hard, clear voice split the air. 'Rosie!'

She turned. Mr Jackson was waiting, his hand out. 'My skates, please!'

Her mother pleaded, 'Couldn't it wait, Mr Jackson. This isn't a good – '

He cut through her. 'I do not want to see this child ever again. My skates, please.' His hand remained rigidly flat, waiting. Rosie bent down to unstrap the skates, sobbing wildly. Looking down, her mother became aware of the savage wound in her daughter's knee.

A stream of blood ran down Rosie's leg. Already the white sock was sodden with it and it was soaking into her trainers. With a gasp her mother dropped to her knees. Fumbling and tugging she unstrapped the skates and handed them to Mr Jackson. He nodded sternly and turned away towards Mrs Scribbins and the still, slumped form of the old man.

Rosie's mother dug into her bag for a scarf and wrapped it gently round her daughter's leg. It stained red instantly. She wound it round twice more and lightly tied a knot.

'Is he . . . is he all right?' sobbed Rosie.

Mrs Scribbins' head jerked up and her mouth snapped open and shut, bird-like. 'Stupid child. Of course he is not all right! You may have killed him. He might die!'

She turned her attention to Rosie's mother. 'Get her out of here. She needs treatment. She's vicious. She should be in a home. This is a police matter!'

Rosie wobbled as her legs struggled to hold her up. She

96

leaned into her mother for support, sobbing continuously. Her mother's arm curled round her and eased her away.

'Don't listen,' she urged. 'Come on. We must get home and do something with your leg. We'll worry about everything else later.'

As they hobbled across the Esplanade to her mother's car they could already hear the strident wail of an ambulance siren in the distance. They had only driven a short way when it hurtled past them in the opposite direction.

Rosie slid down in the seat beside her mother, with the bottom of her sweatshirt clenched in her hands, chewing the edge into a frayed string of cotton.

'Please God,' she whimpered. 'Don't let him die.'

Nine

Once home her mother cleaned her knee and dressed it while Rosie whimpered in an armchair.

After a little while, Harry arrived. He said the old man had been taken to hospital. His condition was not known.

Her mother tucked her into bed, kissed her, drew the curtains and closed the door. Rosie lay and shivered, staring blankly into the ceiling. When her mother returned it was to say that a policewoman had arrived, wanting to talk to Rosie.

Rosie got up and put on a dressing gown. Her tears had left a raw redness around her eyes, but Rosie was expressionless; her shoulders were down and her feet dragged. She would look at neither her mother, nor Harry. Only once did she look up: at the policewoman, who had a kind, tired face. 'Rosie,' she said. 'You might like to know that Mr Blamey, the old man who was hit, is going to be all right. He's shaken up, and he's got some stitches in his head. They'll keep him in hospital for a couple of days but it looks as if he's going to recover.' She smiled at Rosie. She was a young woman and her eyes held no accusation, even when she insisted gently that Rosie should tell everything that happened.

Rosie did. Staring at the floor she went through the whole of the day's events.

The policewoman took notes of everything. 'Mr Scribbins says you weren't aiming at him at all,' she said. 'He says you were deliberately aiming at Mr Blamey who dropped his walking stick by accident.'

Rosie shook her head. 'S'not true.'

'Did anyone else see?' The policewoman looked at Harry and Rosie's mother. They both shook their heads.

'But I did the other time,' said Harry. He explained about the occasion when Mr Scribbins had pushed the wheelchair into Rosie. The policewoman took more notes.

Afterwards she said, 'Mr Scribbins says that was an accident, but Rosie has been trying to get even ever since.'

Rosie didn't even flinch at the lie. All her anger had drained away and she went on staring at the ground. 'S'not true,' she repeated.

The policewoman closed her notebook. 'I may have to come back for a proper statement if Mr and Mrs Scribbins decide to press charges against Rosie.'

Her mother bit her lip and gripped Harry's hand. 'Do you think they will?'

'I'm afraid it's not for me to say.'

She thanked them for their help and Harry and Rosie's mother saw her to the door. Rosie was already on her way back upstairs. She closed the bedroom door and slipped back into bed where she lay on her side.

Mr Jackson was gone forever. He would never forgive her, she knew. Her mother would, and Harry, too. But they would never quite trust her again.

She woke in the morning to the sound of voices raised. Her head ached and her knee was stiff and throbbing. She eased herself over the edge of the bed, keeping the leg straight, and hobbled to her dressing gown.

She found her mother in the kitchen and knew from the sharp sound of the cupboards snapping shut, and the

99

smack of utensils on surfaces, that she was angry. Rosie stood, saying nothing, until her mother sensed her presence and turned.

Her face was set hard and there was a deep frown across her eyes. She stared at Rosie for a moment.

'How are you feeling?'

Rosie shrugged.

'We'll have to change the dressing on that.' She nodded towards Rosie's knee. The bandage was stained through with dried blood. She turned away. 'That was Mr Scribbins at the door.'

'Oh.'

Silence, but for her mother sharply organizing foodstuffs on the shelves.

'He says he's going to sue us unless he gets an apology. He wants an apology and he wants money for all the trouble.' Her voice came faster and more desperate as it poured out all the tension it had stored through the previous evening and the night.

'He wants money to cover his expenses. He says it's going to cost him hundreds of pounds in extra nursing for Mr Blamey, as well as taking him backwards and forwards to hospital. And we've got to pay it or he'll sue us.'

Her voice began to tremble. 'And he says he's going to have you charged with assault and I can't do anything about it because I don't have any money!'

And finally, with her hands covering her face, her shoulders shook and she burst into tears.

'Oh Mum,' cried Rosie. 'I'm sorry. I'm sorry!' She hobbled over and clasped her mother round the waist. With her head pressed into the small of her mother's back she, too, wept.

Twisting round to embrace her daughter, Rosie's

mother recovered, sniffed back the tears, and said, 'You'll have to go and apologize, Rosie. Maybe he'll be different if he sees you really are sorry.'

'But it was all his fault, Mum!'

'Rosie! No matter what he did you can't throw stones like that. Mr Blamey could have been killed. Don't you see how awful it might have been? It would have been . . . it would have been murder! It doesn't matter now who was right or wrong. You must go and apologize.'

'Couldn't I write him a letter? I'll write a proper one. Please . . .'

'No; he wants a personal apology. And Rosie . . .'

'Yes Mum?'

'You'll have to take him your money. Your savings. If he sees you really are trying it might help.'

Rosie was stunned. Her hands went up to her ears to block out the words. 'Mum! Mum! I can't. My skates. I need it for my skates!'

'Rosie, you have to. I know how you feel, but think of Mr Blamey. I don't have any money, and if we don't make some contribution there's no knowing what will happen. We have to try and get Mr Scribbins to change his mind.'

'But the race is on Saturday. I don't have any skates. Mr Jackson's gone and mine are too small.'

'You won't be able to skate on Saturday with your knee.'

'It'll be better – '

'No!' Rosie's mother gripped her by both shoulders and blazed with fury. 'How dare you be so selfish. All this is because of you and your damned skating. You will do as I say and you might as well know now that the skating is over. Over! I've thrown out your old ones. I forbid you to have anything to do with skating again.'

Rosie tore at her mother's dress, pleading, desperate. She shook her head and wept, her voice a plaintive, hopeless cry. 'Oh no, Mum. Please. Please. Let me just try the race. I'll use my old skates. I can still get them on. I must do it. I have to beat the minute. Then I'll give it up. I promise . . .'

Her mother turned away and Rosie folded to the floor, weak and beaten and pleading, but it made no difference.

Her mother had tears in her eyes, but still she said, 'Tomorrow you must go and apologize, and take your money and give it to him. I'm sorry.'

Rosie whimpered, 'He started it; with the walking stick. He just hates me.'

'No-one else saw it as you did. Nobody – in the middle of the Esplanade with everyone watching. Rosie, maybe it's your imagination.'

'But the last time. Harry saw that. He knows . . .'

'Yes, well . . . Harry has his doubts now.'

Rosie sank lower to the floor, curled into a small weak ball and whispered, 'No-one believes me. No-one.' She was left with no strength to get up, nor even to raise her head. Yet somehow she did get up and made her way upstairs to her room where she collapsed on the covers. Her fist went to her mouth and she lay with her teeth pressed to the back of her hand, sucking it for comfort as she had not done since she was a very little girl.

The day passed, and once or twice her mother opened the door and gently asked if she wanted food, or a drink. But Rosie barely even shook her head. Her mother stood worried, poised on the edge of giving way, but then thought better of it.

Later Rosie slept; and her mother returned with a cover which she unfolded carefully over her daughter. She kissed her, stroked her hair and walked quietly away, closing the door behind her.

The next morning was no different. When Rosie awoke it was as if some deep paralysis had gripped her. She stared at the light through the window and knew as she had known in her sleep that there was nothing to get up for. She was beaten. She no longer even cared about the prospect of bowing her head before the triumphant leer of Mr Scribbins. She felt dead inside. Yesterday skating was all that filled her mind; today – nothing. There was to be no more skating and her thoughts were empty, her dreams crushed. She was trapped in a grey numbness. No anger, no bitterness; nothing.

She was still as her mother had left her, under the one cover. She stood up, letting it slide from her, and walked away leaving it where it lay. She went downstairs without washing. Harry was there, sitting at the kitchen table talking to her mother, both drinking coffee. They turned towards her and smiled tired smiles. Rosie seemed hardly to see them.

Harry rose and came over to her. 'Hey, it's not so bad. We'll go to Greece for a couple of weeks and it'll soon be forgotten. Sun, swimming; you won't have time to think about skating.'

Rosie looked at him, neither smiling, nor unsmiling. Her face showed nothing at all. He squatted down so that he could look directly into her eyes. 'It's serious this time Rosie. You could be in big trouble, with the police and everything, unless we do something about it now. I'm sorry.'

'And me, Rosie,' said her mother. 'Honestly; but it will be for the best. You'll see.'

Rosie hardly saw them. 'Do I have to go now?'

Harry sighed. 'Might as well get it over.'

'Do you want one of us to go with you?' asked her mother.

Rosie didn't care. The humiliation of facing Mr Scribbins had no power to move her anymore. She was indifferent to anyone else sharing the moment.

They had already witnessed her destruction on the Esplanade. She wanted no company. She shook her head.

'Have you got your money?'

She shook her head again.

'You get it and I'll put it in an envelope for you,' said her mother.

Rosie turned and trod her way numbly back upstairs to her room to dress. On a shelf was a coffee jar. In the plastic lid a slot had been melted and inside the glass walls was a jumbled pile of coins. She unscrewed the lid, poured it all out onto her bed, and counted. £19.50. Nearly enough. She raised her head and stared out of the window.

Downstairs her mother held open the envelope while Rosie poured in the money. 'I've written a short note to go with it,' said her mother, sealing the envelope.

She smoothed Rosie's hair with her hand and said, 'Just be polite; say you're sorry about Mr Blamey, and hand over the envelope. If he opens it wait until he's read the note and then come away. You don't have to go in or anything.' Her mother squeezed her hand. 'And Rosie, please don't do anything silly.'

She drew Rosie to her, hugged her and added, 'I love you very much.'

Rosie waited until her mother had finished, and turned away. She wished she could hug her in return, but there was no feeling in her; just the numbness. She opened the front door and walked out.

Rosie knew Ailsa Road, where the Scribbinses lived. It

104

was nearly a mile through the town from the seafront. She walked mechanically, her eyes on the ground, not aware of anything around her.

Once in Ailsa Road she could see the sign: the Valley Residential Home for the Elderly. Underneath a motto said: Care and Concern.

She lifted the latch on an enormous green gate and it swung silently open. The Valley was gaunt and tall and dark, like an architect's impression of Mr and Mrs Scribbins themselves. It peered down on her through dark Victorian eyes; large sash windows behind which there was nothing to see but dark wallpaper and dull furniture. On one corner an hexagonal tower rose higher than the adjacent eaves and was topped with a pointed roof, like a witch's hat of grey slates.

The gravelled footpath scrunched under Rosie's feet as she approached the door. The garden was well kept. Neat paths with sharply cut edges branched off and skirted round the corner of the house. Little circles cut in the lawn provided pools of earth for carefully pruned trees that created shadowed glades. Everything was too neat, as if it had been cut out and stuck on. For looking at, not for using.

There were five steps up to the vast green front door. It had panels of coloured glass in it, and coloured glass windows beside it with net curtains in them that made it impossible to see in. Rosie looked for a bell, but there was none. Only a great heavy ring of brass in the middle of the door.

Her heart began to flutter a little. She gripped the envelope and mounted the steps, stretching out her stride for each one. She reached timidly for the knocker and let it fall twice. She had intended to knock gently, but its weight gave it a life of its own, and it fell with a heavy thud that she could hear reverberating through the house.

Then silence. For a second Rosie's spirit lifted as she made believe there was nobody in; that she could turn away with a clear conscience and return to her mother. But then she heard a pattering of feet along the hall, like a skittering of mice, but louder.

She heard the handle turn and the lock mechanism scrape, and the door began to open. First a centimetre of darkness appeared, then two, until the door was open wide enough for the daylight from outside to show the girl, Millie, staring wide-eyed and nervous at her. Behind her everything was gloom and shadow.

'Oh! Oh!' said Millie, birdlike. 'It's you.' She was clutching and tugging at the front of her white apron.

'Hello,' said Rosie. 'Is Mr Scribbins in?'

'You'd better come in.' Millie opened the door wider, stepping aside. Then suddenly she changed her mind. As Rosie stepped forward she narrowed the slot in the open doorway. 'No,' she said breathlessly. 'No; you don't want to come in here. Stay there. Stay there. I'll fetch him. Don't come in.' She bobbed nervously and was gone. Rosie was sorry for the girl. To live in this towering grey building with the Scribbinses for company was appalling to contemplate. No wonder she seemed so timid.

She heard the whining, irritated voice of Mr Scribbins. Involuntarily she found herself backing down two steps. The voice was getting nearer.

The voice was in the hall. '. . . stupid child, disturbing me. How many times must I tell you.' The door was pulled open to reveal the thin frame of Mr Scribbins. He stopped speaking when he saw her. Rosie felt a wave of fear as he loomed over her, the towering distance accentuated by the two steps ahead of her.

She had only ever seen him in an overcoat, and he had looked thin then. Now, in only a shirt and trousers he was skeletal. He was wearing dirty plimsoles and there were stains on his shirt. He had not shaved and a grey and ginger stubble covered his hollow cheeks. His hands were long and the joints were knobbed lumps along each finger. Black hairs grew in the spaces between each joint.

Ten

Rosie swallowed hard, and the words croaked quietly out, 'I've come to apologize.'

A leer spread over his face. 'Just a minute.' He was gone from the doorway, and a few seconds later reappeared. The grim form of his wife stared down on Rosie from over his shoulder. The eyes fixed her hypnotically.

'She says she's come to apologize,' scoffed Mr Scribbins.

The eyes froze Rosie to the spot, or she might have turned and run. 'Well, get on with it then,' hissed Mrs Scribbins.

The words would hardly squeeze themselves from Rosie's stricken throat. 'I'm very sorry for what happened. I've brought this.' She held out the envelope.

Mr Scribbins put his hand to his ear with a theatrical gesture. 'I beg your pardon,' he crowed.

'I said I've brought this,' she held the envelope up a little higher.

'No, the other bit.'

Rosie hung her head. They were really going to make her pay. She had no spirit to retaliate and besides, she couldn't. Her mother had said. She whispered, 'I'm very sorry to have caused you so much trouble – ' A tear started to form in the corner of one eye, but Rosie held it back, praying silently, Don't let me cry. Don't let me. She said again, 'I'm very sorry, sir, to have caused you so much trouble.' She held the envelope out again. 'I've brought this; to help with the bills for Mr Blamey.'

Mr Scribbins reached down the steps and snatched it from her hand. He tore it open, fingered through the money, and read the note Rosie's mother had written. He passed it back for his wife to read.

'She wants us to forgive you,' he scoffed. 'I warned you we'd win. Now we'll make you pay.'

He held up the envelope. 'This isn't compensation. This is a bribe. Wait 'til the police here how you offered us this to stop it going any further. Bribery's an offence.'

Rosie's lips began to tremble. 'Truly, it's not a bribe. Mum thought you wanted compensation. We haven't got any more.'

'We'll have to talk to your mother about it, won't we?' Mr Scribbins gritted his teeth and spat the words out through them. 'Now get out!'

Rosie half-turned to go when she remembered something she had not done; something more important to her than apologizing to the Scribbinses. She stopped.

'Well?' scowled Mr Scribbins.

'I wondered . . . Could I – Could I see Mr Jackson? I wanted to tell him, too, that I'm sorry.'

Mrs Scribbins' head rose higher on her long, thin neck. 'How dare you!' she hissed. 'You have broken that poor man's heart, and you expect him to talk to you? He never wants to set eyes on you again. Go away. Get out!'

Her voice had risen to a shriek, and the two of them seemed to tower over her. It was more than she could stand and she backed, stumbling, down the steps.

She would have fled down the gravel path immediately, but a sudden crash stopped her in mid stride.

At the far end of the house, at first floor level, a window pane burst outwards. Shards of glass showered down on to the lawn and the gravel path. As Rosie looked up she saw Millie at an adjacent first floor window. In one hand she held a balled handkerchief, and she was biting on it nervously.

In the other she waved a piece of paper. She seemed to be waving it at Rosie. The Scribbinses didn't see Millie as she stepped back into the shadows of the darkened room.

Mr Scribbins had moved further out of the porch and looked up at the broken window. He murmured some instructions back to his wife, who turned on her heel and was gone.

Rosie was bewildered. She made a move towards the scattered glass, but the voice of Mr Scribbins stopped her. 'Mind your own business. Get out. You're in enough trouble as it is.' He was down beside her, one hand roughly gripping the top of her arm. 'Unless you want to explain to the police why you broke a window.'

He gave her a shove and she stumbled forward, grateful for the chance to escape. She closed the gate behind her. Looking back she saw Mrs Scribbins standing at the broken window, looking down.

Rosie walked home slowly, confused. What did the broken window mean? How had it happened? If the old people at the home were in wheelchairs how could they have done it? And why? None of them looked as if they had the strength. Mr Jackson, she reflected, would have the strength. His arms were tough from wheeling himself. Perhaps it was Millie. That would explain her nervousness. But why was she waving? Maybe she was appealing to Rosie for help.

Rosie shuddered. She could understand the horror of facing alone the wrath of the Scribbinses. That was probably what had made Millie the way she was.

By the time Rosie arrived home the grey emptiness had

settled on her once more. The race was only five days away and she was to be robbed of it. She expected Bernard would win it, but never in the minute. She knew he could skate well enough to win; but she knew, too, that he could never do it as fast as she. But Rosie would never be able to say so, for she would never be able to prove it. No-one would ever believe her.

No-one would ever believe her, either, about the Scribbinses' smashed window. She decided to say nothing about it to her mother, nor to Harry.

Next day Rosie returned to school where children stood in groups and looked at her while they whispered together about her being in trouble with the police.

On Wednesday the policewoman came again and took a proper statement from Rosie.

She was very serious about it all and Rosie expected the worst, but she was too numb to care much about what happened. She withdrew into herself, blocking out the excitement that was mounting all around her as children on roller-skates practised everywhere.

Her mother worried about her. Rosie grew thinner, and her eyes seemed to have shrunk in their sockets. Nothing could be done or said to bring out the old, bright Rosie.

After school each day she went straight to her room, did her homework, and then sat staring at the wall, or out of the window into the street below, her mind blunted and empty.

Her mother called her down for tea; special teas of Rosie's favourite foods, but she only picked them over and left them.

'I'm not hungry,' she said, and went back to her room to stare listlessly on the world outside.

It was on Thursday evening, at the window, that she

111

saw a figure she recognized walking down the street; and for the first time since the Scribbinses window had crashed in pieces to the ground, her interest was aroused.

It was Millie.

She was on the opposite side of the road, coming timidly down past garden walls and hedges. At every step she darted a nervous glance behind her and to all sides, and as she walked she tugged nervously at the bib of the apron she still wore. Her lips worked unconsciously. Her head darted out and she studied garden gates and doors on each side of the road. She was looking for a number.

When she was opposite Rosie's garden she stopped. By now Rosie was keenly interested. Her head was up off her arms, waiting for Millie's next move. Darting her head to left and right Millie scuttled across the road to Rosie's gate and waited there, hopping from one foot to the other, tugging, biting her lip.

Rosie tapped on the window to the girl below. She banged harder. Millie looked up and saw her and for a moment relief appeared in a smile on her face, and then was gone.

She darted more glances up and down the road and beckoned desperately to Rosie. Come down. Come down.

Rosie frowned and pointed a finger at herself. Millie nodded. Rosie took the stairs two at a time in her stockinged feet, quietly. She could hear Harry and her mother in the sitting room. Carefully she opened the front door, and leaving it ajar ran out to the gate.

Millie was waiting, nervous as ever. 'I shouldn't be here. I shouldn't,' she wailed. 'He made me.'

'Who?' asked Rosie. 'Millie, don't worry. What's the matter?'

'They'll lock me up if they find out. I don't like being locked up. I have to go.' Millie's eyes were wide and frightened. Rosie felt a tug of pity for the girl, whose simple face carried so much fear.

From the pocket of her apron bib she plucked a folded sheet of paper. 'He said I had to give you this.'

'Who, Millie, who?'

'Mr Jackson.'

Rosie unfolded the paper. Hurriedly scribbled were the words: 'Must see you. Need help.' and the initials CPJ.

C for Charles; J for Jackson, thought Rosie.

She gripped Millie's arm and the timid creature leapt with fright. 'Millie; I'm not going to hurt you. When did he give you this?'

'Don't tell 'em. Please don't tell 'em. I'll get into awful trouble.' —

'I promise I won't tell. Please. When . . .?'

'When he broke the window.'

'So it was him who broke the window!'

Millie nodded. 'He scribbled the note and told me to sneak it to you when you left; but then he heard you going too soon, so he broke the window. He thought it would delay you. But it was too late, anyway.

'He kept telling me to bring it here, but I've been too frightened.'

Rosie opened the gate and beckoned Millie through. 'Come with me,' she said. 'We've got to show this to my mum. She'll know what to do.'

Millie was horror-struck. 'No; I can't. I 'ave to get back. You don't know what they'll do. They mustn't know I've been here.' She backed away down the street.

'You were a beautiful skater, Rosie,' she blurted. 'Like a ballet dancer. I wish I could do it.' And she turned and fled.

Rosie began to call after her, but instead her arms fell to her side. Poor simple Millie; she was terrified of the

Scribbinses. It wasn't fair to frighten her any further. And besides, what good would it do? It all probably had some simple explanation. Or it might be a trap set by the Scribbinses. She shivered as she remembered her visit to the house. Poor Millie!

But there was still the note, in an old man's writing, hurriedly scribbled: 'Must see you. Need help. CPJ.'

Rosie fingered the paper thoughtfully, retracing her steps up the path to the door. She closed it behind her.

'Is that you, Rosie?' Her mother appeared at the sitting room door. 'I didn't hear you go out.' She studied her daughter's face. 'Problem?'

'I just got this note. Millie brought it.'

'Who's Millie?'

'The girl who works for the Scribbinses.'

A look flicked across her mother's face; suspicious perhaps, sceptical. It was there and gone again quick as a blink. 'Oh . . . where is she now?'

'She ran off. She wouldn't stay. She was frightened.' Rosie had not caught the scepticism in her mother's voice. She offered the note. Her mother read it.

'It's from Mr Jackson,' said Rosie.

Her mother was silent; and in the silence it dawned on Rosie what she was thinking.

'I didn't write it! Millie brought it. She said Mr Jackson wrote it when I went round with the money. It was him that smashed the window. Honest!'

'What window?'

Weakly Rosie remembered she had kept it a secret.

Harry appeared in the doorway behind her mother. 'Rosie,' he said softly, 'how can we believe this after everything else that has happened?'

'Why should you think I would lie? You didn't the first time when Scribbins ran into me with the wheelchair.

114

Why now? Mr Jackson is in trouble. I know it. And we ought to be helping him. You're just frightened of old Scribbins.'

The rising tide of hysteria in Rosie's voice was cut short by the sound of a sharp crack as her mother's hand swept across Rosie's cheek. A crimson patch spread there, and Rosie was silent; shocked. It was the first time she could ever remember her mother hitting her.

'I've had enough, Rosie; I really have. I'm beginning to think you must be mad. This obsession with the Scribbinses. It's the skating, I know. I blame myself, but you have got to learn . . .'

Colour had risen in both Rosie's cheeks. On the one side it was caused by her mother's slap; but on the other it was the rising tide of anger. 'You pig!' she screamed.

Never before had she spoken in such a way to her mother; but she didn't hear the words she was using, her rage was so great. Her mother's hand swung out again with a stinging crack, and this time a sob choked in Rosie's throat.

'Get upstairs,' said her mother grimly. 'Get to bed and don't come down. I want an apology in the morning.'

Rosie hurled herself past her mother and up the stairs. She slammed shut her bedroom door and flung herself down on the bed, punching at the pillow, growling with a savage fury she couldn't control. She hated everyone. How dare they believe a man like Scribbins before her!

Well, tomorrow they would learn. If they wouldn't help, then she would do it alone. Whatever the note meant; whether it was a trap or a real call for help, she would defy them all, whatever the consequences.

115

Eleven

Rosie woke the next morning to the sound of her mother vacuuming in the room below. Friday. Her mother always vacuumed the dining room on a Friday. A school morning. Rosie leapt out of bed immediately, jaw hard-set with stubborn determination.

She strode purposefully into the bathroom, scrubbed at her face, brushed her teeth mercilessly. Back in her room she threw on her schoolclothes. She packed her school bag, took a deep breath and descended the stairs.

Her mother was putting away the cleaner when she appeared. She shut the cupboard door and said with a smile, 'Morning, young lady.'

'Morning.' Rosie strode past to the kitchen.

'Haven't you got something to say to me?'

Rosie opened and shut cupboards, slamming bowl and muesli packet, sugar, spoon. She sat down, concentrating on filling her bowl and pouring milk. She shook her head firmly.

Her mother sighed. 'Well, that's a pity. Unless you apologize there will be no trip to Greece. Harry and I agreed last night. And as there is no-one I can leave you with – especially now, after all this – it will mean that if you don't go, none of us can. I hope you feel good about it.'

Rosie shrugged her shoulders. 'Don't care.'

Her mother heaved another heavy sigh and turned wearily away.

When Rosie finished her breakfast she washed up her bowl and spoon and dried them, slamming and banging noisily at this cupboard and that. She snatched up her bag and strode past her mother to the door.

''Bye,' she called curtly.

'Rosie,' called her mother. Rosie kept heading for the door.

'Rosie!' came the call again, sharply. Rosie stopped and her mother strode over to her. 'Rosie, don't do this. It's not fair. Since when have you not kissed me goodbye, even in a bad mood?'

Rosie wouldn't look up.

'Rosie, please.'

Reluctantly she raised her head, and as her mother lowered her cheek Rosie brushed it carelessly with her lips; as little a kiss as she could possibly make it. For a moment she felt the urge to drop her bag and throw her arms round her mother's neck, but she checked herself despite the ache of desolation she felt inside. She was saddened by the misery she saw on her mother's face, but she dared not soften her resolve.

'Goodbye, my darling,' said her mother.

'Bye, mum,' said Rosie, more gently this time. She walked out of the door and away down the path feeling more alone than she could remember in her life before.

It was early for school, but her mother hadn't noticed because Rosie had always been early leaving the house, usually so she could get a little practice time at the Esplanade. She followed the usual route until she reached a corner where the road branched away in the direction of Ailsa Road. She stood and checked there was no-one to notice she had gone a different way; no school friends, nor teachers. Once satisfied she set off quickly on the road to The Valley Residential Home for the Elderly.

She reached the heavy green gate. On the other side nothing in the garden stirred nor – from what she could see – in the house. Only one thing had changed. Over the first floor window a sheet of brown cardboard covered one pane, where it had been smashed. Everything else was as gaunt and dark as before.

Not quite everything. High up in the hexagonal tower on the corner of the house, at a top, third floor window, a white sign in the window said simply, 'HELP.'

It hadn't been there before; Rosie was certain. Anyone who studied the building as she had done would have noticed it immediately. She set her jaw firmly, opened the gate, and marched down the scrunching gravel path. Her heart was pounding by the time she reached the door. And she wondered with a fluttering heart what she was doing there on the steps of the awful house.

The knocker was in her hand. She hesitated, and then: bang, bang, bang; three times the echoing thud boomed through the house. Once again she heard the mouse-like pitter-patter of Millie's feet. The door swung slowly open. Millie saw Rosie and her eyes popped. Rosie smiled. Millie emitted a squeak and backed away.

'Well, girl, who is it?' came the thin, spidery voice of Mrs Scribbins. Millie jumped at the sound.

'Please Missis; please – it's – it's Rosie Swallow.'

Mrs Scribbins was at the door, hawk-like eyes fixing Rosie with a gleaming stare.

She said nothing, waiting. Behind her Rosie could see Millie chewing on a knuckle and shaking her head, wide-eyed and terrified. For a second or two Rosie's courage nearly failed her, but she gazed defiantly back at the beaklike nose and said, 'I've come to see Mr Jackson.'

'But Mr Jackson has no wish to see you,' came the thin voice from between thin lips.

'I – I've got to,' replied Rosie. 'I'm not going.'

Mrs Scribbins studied her for a moment or two, then a grin spread across her mouth. It touched only her mouth, and there was no humour in it, only malice. Rosie did not know if it was meant to terrify her, this grin, but it certainly did. Her legs quailed.

Mrs Scribbins stepped aside from the doorway. 'Very well,' she said. 'Since you are so insistent you had better come in.'

The bottom dropped out of Rosie's stomach. She had not expected to be invited in. Now that it had happened she realized that the last thing she wanted was to join Millie and Mr Jackson and all the frail, frightened faces on the other side of that door. But she remembered the note from Mr Jackson and the white sign in the window calling for help. She recovered and began to climb the steps.

She got to the door and was passing through it when Mrs Scribbins pounced on her.

'Got you!' she crowed. 'I ought to lock you up until the police get here.'

Her large hooked nose was pushed up close to Rosie's. Her fingers were as hard as talons, the nails biting into Rosie's arm. 'How would you like that, hey? Interfering little busybody.'

Rosie could not reply. Her throat was closed and dry and her lips were frozen. All colour had drained from her face.

Mrs Scribbins dragged her down the steps, Rosie stumbling at every one. She dragged her back along the gravel path. When they reached the gate, she threw up the latch, flung open the gate, and hurled Rosie down on to the pavement outside.

'And this afternoon your mother shall hear about this,'

she spat. 'And the police. How dare you harass us; and these poor, helpless old people. Leave us alone!' She slammed the gate shut and strode back to the house.

She stood there, watching Rosie pick herself up, bandaged knee smarting terribly. Rosie limped out of sight of the door and paused to catch her breath.

Although she was out of sight of the door, the window of the tower was still visible high above. She could see the sign with HELP in big, bold letters. She gasped. Beside it, propped painfully on one elbow inside the window, was Mr Jackson. He was peering out, trying to force open the window with one hand. Gradually it slipped up.

Rosie waved to him. He was too busy with the sash to notice. She waved again. Gradually the window came open until the gap was wide enough for him to get his head through. He did so, and forced it open further with his back, clinging to the sill with both hands.

'He's out of his wheelchair,' thought Rosie. 'He'll fall.'

She waved again as Mr Jackson looked up, and he saw her. Instead of calling out he put his finger to his lips and beckoned her forward.

'What's the matter?' she called. Abruptly he waved her to silence, urging her to approach.

Rosie crept quietly back to a point where she could see the front door. It was closed. There was no sign of anyone. Carefully, favouring her good knee, she climbed the wall and crept through the hedges and the perfectly trimmed shrubs until she was under the tower.

Mr Jackson hissed down to her, 'Thank God you came.'

She hissed back, 'What's the matter? Why are we whispering?'

'No time for all that, Rosie. You were right. We were all wrong. They're mad. Quite mad. We're all prisoners here.' The words came hissing down to her in an urgent whisper across three floors. They sounded so loud. She looked around. No-one was about.

'All prisoners,' continued Mr Jackson. 'They intimidate the old people into signing over everything they own to them. Either that or they ill-treat them until they die. They've all told me.'

'As soon as I arrived they tried it on me. Bit off more than they could chew. Been a prisoner since. Smashed a window and they moved me up here where I can't do any harm.'

A steely smile spread over his face. 'They don't know Charles Jackson, hm? Rosie; you must get help. Immediately. They are planning something; I don't know what. But you must tell the authorities.'

For the first time Rosie realized her heart was pounding. Her arms and legs shook.

'Can't I get you out?' she called back.

He held up a finger to silence her. 'No. We've been lucky. Much more of this and someone will hear us. Even Millie is terrified. I don't know if we can trust her.'

'She brought me the note.'

'Good-o. But Rosie; now it's up to you. Go to the police station. Tell them I sent you.'

Rosie was already moving away when the impossibility of their situation dawned on her. She stopped.

'Go on. Go on, girl.'

'It's no good,' she called up, dully.

'What d'you mean, no good?'

'They won't believe me. They all think I'm trying to be spiteful to the Scribbinses. They've done a good job, the pair of them,' she said ruefully, 'Nobody believes anything I say anymore.'

She looked up. 'It won't work. I know it won't.' She

took a deep breath, and swallowed down the sick feeling in her stomach. 'I'll have to come and get you.'

'It's too dangerous. They really are mad. You mustn't. There's no knowing what they'll do.'

'I'm not leaving you here. Is there a back way?'

He nodded. 'I'll try and get back to my wheelchair.'

Rosie moved off towards the rear of the house when he called her back, hissing her name, 'Rosie.'

She stopped, looked up.

'Please forgive me; for everything,' he said.

She grinned at him, and vanished out of sight.

Twelve

At the back of the house Rosie came to a wide asphalt drive. Good for skating, she thought absurdly. The drive led in one direction to a pair of open gates that formed a rear exit to the road. In the other direction they led to a garage built into the back of the house. It had a wide up-and-over door, big enough for two cars. The door was closed, but she could hear noises the other side of it: tools being used, muffled voices, and a roaring sound she couldn't place.

She crept past the closed garage door. Beyond it was the back door to the house. It was open.

She crept in. Further down, on the left, was a doorway through which she could hear the voices clearly. It was the inside door to the garage, connecting it to the house, and it was open.

Further off down the passage she could see another, half-glazed door, and through that the foot of the stairs was visible. She guessed they would lead her to Mr Jackson.

She trod quietly forward. The voices were clearer still, but she could think of no safe way of crossing the doorway to the garage.

Over the roaring noise, that still she could not identify, came Mrs Scribbins' reedy voice: 'She won't be back. I frightened her witless. But hurry up; that old fool upstairs will spoil everything.'

The thin whine of Mr Scribbins replied, 'Just one more . . . got it. There. Hold this while I get up.'

Rosie heard the sound of Mr Scribbins dragging himself up from the floor. She listened as he clapped the dust out of his clothes. He sounded smug as he said, 'He won't spoil anything after today, my love. We'll take Mr Jackson for a nice little drive – '

'But he won't come for a drive with us.'

'Just listen woman! We'll say we no longer wish to have him here; we're taking him back to his hotel. He'll think we're fools, because he can go straight to the police as soon as he's free and tell them everything. But,' emphasized Mr Scribbins, 'we won't take him anywhere of the sort. We'll take him for a drive. To the top of Salcombe Hill to admire the view.'

Rosie could not see the car, nor the Scribbinses; but the conversation was too easy to follow. Her eyes were widening with horror.

Mr Scribbins continued, 'And now I've finished with the car, it has a few problems. Oh, nothing anyone could detect. But when we park on the cliff-top I'll forget to set the handbrake, and the car will start to roll forward.

'And when I press the footbrake it won't work – don't worry yourself about the details.' He waved aside any argument. 'I know what I'm doing. Just take my word for it, the footbrake won't work.

'Then I'll snatch on the handbrake; but with only one strand of wire left – ping! It'll snap in two.'

'Suppose it doesn't?'

'Just leave it to me. A good, hard yank – it'll snap all right. And the car will just keep rolling. We'll be all right. We can jump for it. But poor old Jackson . . . I'm afraid he'll be straight over the cliff, two hundred metres into the sea.'

Rosie was stunned. Mr Jackson was right. They were insane. She tried to shake what she was hearing out of her ears. She had to get by the doorway. She had to get Mr Jackson out. There was no time to lose. She crept forward and peered round the door jamb. They were admiring their handiwork, with their backs to Rosie. A green station wagon was standing before them. It was the one Mr Jackson had talked about, specially modified to take wheelchairs. There were no back seats and the roof had been raised slightly.

On a workbench stood a blow-lamp, alight and roaring out a blue flame. It was the noise she had not been able to place. Mr Scribbins must have used the blow-lamp to tamper with the brakes.

The Scribbinses still had their backs to her. She crept forward. But as she did so she failed to notice that in the passageway a wall light was on. It threw her shadow into the garage, over the Scribbinses and on to the car, where they saw it. The pair wheeled round to see Rosie framed in the doorway, frozen with fear.

'You fool,' squealed Mr Scribbins at his wife. 'I thought you said she'd gone. Get her!'

As Mr Scribbins leapt forward Rosie's senses returned. She dived past the doorway just as he reached it. She flung herself down the passageway and wrenched open the glass-topped door.

She heard Mr Scribbins call back to his wife, 'Go round the front. Cut her off.' Rosie was through the door. She heard the pounding of feet behind her. Without looking back she slammed shut the door. There was a crash and a scream of pain.

She glanced behind to see Mr Scribbins with his arm completely through the glass pane. The window was smashed and blood poured from his hand. He struggled at the catch with the other, whimpering and cursing.

Rosie was about to start up the stairs when she realized it was hopeless. Once up the stairs there was no escape. He would be too close behind.

She ran on. The house echoed her tread. It was full of side doors and passageways, but she dared not trust any of them to lead her to safety. Scribbins was already through the door, trailing blood behind him as he stumbled forward.

Rosie turned a corner. She was in the main hall. Ahead of her was the front door. She remembered Mrs Scribbins outside, heading to cut her off. She heard a whimper nearby. In a corner, half hidden from view, was the terrified Millie.

Rosie ran to her. 'Quickly,' she said. 'Is there another way out?'

Millie trembled, wide-eyed and silent.

Rosie shook her. 'Millie,' she pressed. 'Which way? I have to know.'

Millie pointed to the front door. 'That's the only way.'

Rosie dashed forward and heaved the door open just as Mr Scribbins appeared behind her in the hall. He lunged at her, flinging out his good arm. She ducked through the door and threw it shut behind her. Again she heard Mr Scribbins scream with pain as it slammed against his wrist.

She was racing for the front gate when a voice stopped her. 'Rosie!'

It was Mr Jackson, still at the window. He threw down a bundle. 'They'll catch you before you get a hundred yards. Get those on. It's your only chance.'

It was the old soiled bundle with the skates. She plucked hold of one end and let the skates tumble clattering to the ground.

There was no-one in sight. The front door was still ajar, but the only sound from behind it was Mr Scribbins choking with pain. She dived behind a shrub as she heard the rapid scrunching of gravel from the side of the house. Mrs Scribbins came like a vampire searching for prey.

Rosie prayed that her breath might come more silently as she lay still, hidden from view. She could see the black stockinged feet in their black shoes pass by.

Carefully, quietly, she sat up and fixed first one, then the other skate to her feet, buckling the straps, holding her breath every time a buckle jingled against metal.

Finally it was done. In her concentration she had lost track of the Scribbinses. She could hear nothing. No sound from the door. No sound from the garden. She listened. Silence.

No, not quite silence. She heard a sniffing; a sad whimpering. She glanced up at the window. No sign of Mr Jackson. She hoped he had not fallen back. Still the whimpering went on. Millie's whimpering.

The front door swung slowly open. Millie peered round it. 'Rosie,' she whispered urgently. 'Rosie.'

Rosie crept out from behind the shrub. 'Here.'

'It's – it's all right, Rosie. They've gone round the back. You can get Mr Jackson now.'

Rosie crept forward. The skates crunched on the gravel path.

'Quickly,' called Millie.

Rosie ran forward. The wheels wouldn't turn on the stones. Rosie carefully climbed the steps, holding on to the sides so that she wouldn't lose her balance.

She was on the top step when the door was flung wide open. Scribbins was standing inside it. One hand, covered in blood, gripping Millie's hair.

Rosie darted a glance over her shoulder. Mrs Scribbins

had appeared on the steps behind her, blocking the path out. On roller-skates, on the steps, Rosie was helpless.

Mr Scribbins' face was scarlet with rage. One hand hung by his side. The wrist where it had been smashed in the door was purple and swelling. The other hand gripped Millie's hair, smearing blood there. Millie wept copiously. 'I'm sorry, Rosie. He made me. He made me,' she wept.

As she spoke Mrs Scribbins struck from the steps. Like a black snake she pounced and her hand drove down into Rosie's shoulder, making her wince with pain. She forced her through the open door.

'I'm sorry, Rosie,' wept Millie.

'Don't worry, Millie. It'll be all right. You'll see,' Rosie comforted.

The door slammed shut behind them and Rosie quaked. Mr Scribbins' bleeding hand lashed across her face.

'Look at me,' he screamed. 'Look what you've done to me.' He was frothing at the mouth in his rage.

'Get her in the car,' he snapped at his wife. 'Get her in the car and stay with her. I'll get Jackson.'

He pushed Millie before him. 'Get up those stairs.'

Rosie was marched roughly back through the passage towards the garage. The skates made it difficult for her to balance. She knew that unless she could win one second's release from the grip she would never escape.

Mrs Scribbins pushed her on through the shattered glazed door and the open garage door beyond, towards the car.

The blowlamp, still burning, stood on a bench, just out of reach. A wild idea came to Rosie. A few more inches; just a few.

Under the pressure of the vice-like hand she let the skates slip from under her. She crashed down on her injured knee. Sweat beaded out of her forehead as the pain sliced through her.

'Get up,' screamed Mrs Scribbins. She kicked roughly at Rosie, who climbed painfully to her feet. Now, though, she was a few inches further to one side, and the blowlamp was closer. Rosie lunged at it. For a second she thought she had missed, but her fingers hooked inside the handle, and it was in her grasp.

She swept it round and pressed the barrel against the wrist that held her. She smelled her own hair burning, but a howl of pain from Mrs Scribbins told her it had worked. The hand released her for the vital second.

Rosie ducked away from Mrs Scribbins, still holding the blowlamp. She hurled herself towards the door; but Mrs Scribbins was already recovering. She grabbed a can that stood nearby; a large, heavy oil can, and flung it.

It hit Rosie behind the knees and sent her sprawling across the garage floor towards the passageway. Her knee seared a scar into her mind, and her temple smacked sickeningly into the door frame. Still she scrambled up. Mrs Scribbins lunged, but Rosie ducked through the doorway, sliding and stumbling on her skates.

From down the passageway she heard a hoarse cry of alarm. Mr Scribbins had heard the commotion and had come to investigate. Millie was behind him, rigid with fear.

Rosie fled down the passageway to the back door. She slammed into it, skates spinning, and as she wrenched at the handle she glanced back. Mrs Scribbins was about to throw the can.

There was no time to get through the door. Rosie had only one weapon. The blowlamp was still in her hand. She flung it. It was not a good throw, but it was enough.

129

It ricocheted off the wall and bounced down the passage-way towards the Scribbinses. The retaliation caught Mrs Scribbins off guard. She dropped the can. It hit the ground and split open. It had not been very full, but what contents there were spilled out and ran down the corridor towards Rosie.

'That's not oil,' squealed Mr Scribbins in alarm. 'It's petrol – '

Before he could finish a thin stream of the liquid reached the blowlamp. There was a fluttering whisp of vapour and a flash. Rosie was flung against the wall, a dull boom aching in her ears. She heard Millie scream far back down the corridor. In an instant a wall of blue flame had cut her off from the Scribbinses. Through the flames she saw them retreating into the garage.

'Millie,' screamed Rosie over the roar of flame. 'Get out. Run. Get the old people out. Hurry!'

Millie was frozen, uncomprehending.

Once more Rosie screamed, 'Millie!' The sound ripped out of her throat. Millie came to life, turned on her heel and fled from view.

Once more Rosie struggled with the door, wrenched it open, and flung herself outside. Turning, she watched in horror as the garage door rode up on its hinges. Mrs Scribbins was already in the station wagon behind the driving wheel, eyes narrowed, lips drawn back, revving the engine.

Rosie launched herself down the asphalt drive towards the open double gates and the road. Even as she did so the car leapt forward, while Mr Scribbins flung himself into the passenger seat, slamming the door shut.

Rosie reached the road first, with the car bumper at her heel. She grabbed at the gatepost and swivelled herself tightly round it into the street. The car, unable to turn so acutely, shot out into the road. A horn blared and a van swerved to avoid the station wagon as it careered out of the driveway and stalled halfway up the kerb on the far side of the road.

Rosie didn't wait to see what happened next. She flung herself forward, head and knees aching, hair scorched, legs trembling. She skated and stumbled and ran on the uneven pavements. She heard a screech of wheels, and the Scribbins' car was flying down the road towards her.

A grey despair began to envelope Rosie. It was only a matter of time before her clumsy stumbling destroyed her. This was her last chance.

'You must skate,' she scolded herself. 'Skate!'

Breathing first, fix the breathing. Mr Jackson's words came back. Her breath was more even; and as her breath came under control not only did the skating come easier, but her fear diminished, too. Now legs; legs and arms together; head down. Through the desperate urgency and the vision of the flames boiling up behind her in the passageway she heard the echo of Mr Jackson's words on the Esplanade: 'If you panic you are lost.'

Her legs began to feel good, despite the bandaged knee. They powered backwards, driving her body on, low and weaving. She was aware of lampposts, trees, pedestrians. They were all a blur, and behind her the station wagon came relentlessly on. The gap had closed to inches but still they couldn't catch her.

Rosie could feel the squares of pavement bumping under her feet. 'It's slowing me down,' she thought. 'I need asphalt. The road . . .'

With a glance behind she leapt from the pavement over the kerb stones and into the road, just centimetres ahead of the Scribbins' car. Only one thought was in Rosie's mind: the beach; I'm safe on the beach.

131

They couldn't follow her there, and Harry would be setting out his deckchairs. Her stomach felt dead as she remembered the flames and Mr Jackson, helpless three floors up. But she dared not stop.

Rosie was tiring. They were in the High Street now, the Esplanade only a few hundred metres away, but her legs trembled and her knee was a fierce pain that threaded up to her hip.

The rhythm kept her going; driving, driving with her legs. Once she kicked backwards and heard the clang of her skate on the bumper of the chasing station wagon, but still she kept on.

She was no longer aware of anything around her. It had all blended into a blur of speed and noise, when above it all she heard a scream, 'Look out!'

She looked up. The burning heat of her breath in her chest turned cold. She had forgotten the road works. Fore Street was blocked by workmen and equipment. There was no way through. She was bearing down on it at breathtaking speed. There was no time even to think. A workman pushed a flat trolley out into the road, oblivious of the disaster that approached. Rosie saw it just in time. She leapt, landed cleanly on the flat surface of it, and shot off the other side, never breaking rhythm for an instant.

The workman leapt to safety as the Scribbinses bore down. They smashed into the trolley, sending it crashing through a shop window. The station wagon hit the kerb, steadied itself, and rushed on. The gap had been widened. But Mr Scribbins was triumphant. He, too, had seen the road works. 'We've got her,' he crowed. 'She's ours.'

But Rosie had not slowed down. There was one way out. A lunatic chance, but she knew that if she gave in now, all was lost. She summoned her final reserves of

132

strength and with one last sprinting rush she flung herself at the roadworks.

The lorry was still there. The digger had been taken off for the day's work, but the planks down which they lowered it were still in position. Rosie lined up on one of them. She heard a low gasp of horror from the workmen as she approached. She ignored it all, everything; never taking her eyes from the lip of the boards where they met the ground. The wind was singing past her as she hit one of them. She bobbed, her feet lifted onto the board, and she was climbing. Both feet held together, barely narrower than the plank they were on. Rosie crouched down, gripping her knees, her mind spreading out and through her whole body, feeling the skates, feeling every mark on the plank, concentrating.

She climbed higher, higher. In less than a second she had sped to the raised end of the board which pointed out across the Esplanade and seaward like the barrel of a cannon; and like a cannonball she shot from the end.

She saw the front of the lorry far, far below her as she shot into the air. For one sickening, fleeting moment she wobbled, threatening to capsize, but her arms shot out as balances; and suddenly she was not Rosie, but a magical, flying thing; a creature from another dimension, detached, suspended, watching. She soared high over the Esplanade, hearing no sounds. There were only the faces of the people below, struck dumb as she floated overhead. There was Harry, mouth open, frozen in mid-stride, deckchair in hands.

And as she watched, mysteriously suspended, free as a bubble, the scene below her seemed gradually to come to life. The streets sounds began to reach up and whisper to her; like a frozen film speeding up the people and the traffic seemed to quicken their pace. She was drifting

133

down; closer, closer. The air hissed past her as she plunged in a long, ripping arc to the ground.

She lost her nerve, and as the stack of deckchairs loomed larger and larger she screamed, 'Harry!'

In the brief flick of time it took for the word to leave her lips she smashed into one side of the deckchair stack, spun round, crashed into Harry and sent them both plummeting off the edge of the Esplanade on to the pebbles below.

The Scribbinses had watched Rosie's heedless plunge into the roadworks, up and over the planks, with fascination. They were hypnotized by her flight, unaware that they, too, were thundering along the same path. In the few moments that it took Rosie to lift in the air and plunge out of sight it was too late for them.

'Brake!' screamed Mr Scribbins, 'For God's sake, brake!'

His wife pumped furiously at the brake pedal. 'It doesn't work,' she frothed. Her eyes widened as she turned to meet her husband's terrified gaze. They had forgotten their tampering with the brakes. In the dash out of the garage and through the town the footbrakes had finally been squeezed clean of hydraulic fluid. Now they were empty and there was nothing, nothing at all, that could be done to make them function.

In her panic Mrs Scribbins pressed the throttle pedal to the floor. The car accelerated, landing squarely with one set of wheels on each plank, and roared forward.

They had already hit the planks before Mr Scribbins could grab for the handbrake and snatch it up. It came up solid for a moment, then went loose – useless. He yanked it up once, twice. Nothing. The last wire strand, that he had left for their plot against Mr Jackson, had parted.

The car followed Rosie into the air. People scattered

from under it as it nosed into view over the back of the lorry. It was right behind Rosie, soaring overhead, then plummeting down. But the extra burst of speed as Mrs Scribbins stamped on the throttle, and the wide expanse of the vehicle's underside acting like a kite, helped to keep it airborne.

It soared further out than Rosie, bounced on the top of the deckchair stack, and nosedived over the edge of the Esplanade into the pebbles where it hung vertically for two long seconds before toppling over, on to its roof.

But Rosie never knew. She lay very close to unconsciousness, on top of the dumbstruck Harry who was lying winded where he had broken her fall. Rosie's arm swung loose at a strange angle from the elbow, but she raised herself up and mumbled to Harry, 'Fire. Mr Jackson, others. Burning. Hurry.'

The fierce pain in her arm, her knee and her head burned itself out in the blackness of oblivion, and she sank back into Harry's shoulder.

Thirteen

Rosie woke briefly to a faint light and the murmur of voices, and subsided again into a sleep full of pain. Her arm was being seared by flame and all around her were the laughing heads of the Scribbinses, floating bodiless, and Mr Jackson trying to talk, but no words coming.

A solid scene came to her of the yellow flame exploding through the hallway, and Mr Jackson calling out to her through the erupting fire.

Her eyes opened with a start and she cried out, 'Fire!'

'Rosie, Rosie, it's all right.' It was her mother speaking.

Rosie was in a hospital bed, and a pale yellow sunlight was forcing its way through the closed curtains. Her mother gripped her hand. Rosie's other arm was wrapped and bandaged against her body. Behind her mother stood Harry. Both peered down at her with deeply furrowed brows etching their concern upon their faces.

Rosie's eyes swivelled in their sockets as, disorientated, she wondered how she had got there. Then faster than thought the past came back to her: the fire, the chase, her leap to the beach; then nothing.

She pushed herself upright, eyes wide. The pain in her right arm made her gasp and she cried out, 'Mr Jackson.'

'Shhh. He's all right, Rosie. Mr Jackson's well. He's safe. Lie still.' Her mother leaned forward and gently drew Rosie's head towards her, pressing it cheek to cheek. Rosie relaxed in the warmth and soft perfume of it.

Her mother drew away and looked keenly but softly

into Rosie's eyes. 'They were all saved: Mr Jackson, eight others, and Millie. They were very frightened but they are safe now. The fire brigade couldn't save the house. It's gone.'

Rosie opened her mouth to speak, but her mother gently touched her fingers to Rosie's lips.

'Mrs Scribbins is dead,' she said quietly. 'She broke her neck when the car followed you on to the beach. Mr Scribbins broke both legs and is cut up pretty badly.'

Rosie flopped back on the pillows. Dead! Her mind whirled. Dead! She hadn't expected anyone to die. She felt a creeping chill run through her. They would blame her . . .

Her mother was gently squeezing her hand. 'Rosie, Millie has told everything. The police have the whole story; from her and Mr Jackson and the others.'

Rosie shuddered, nodding, and closed her eyes, sighing with relief.

'Rosie.' Her mother's voice was a whisper.

Rosie looked. There were tears bubbling over in her mother's eyes.

'Rosie, please forgive me. You were right. All the time you were in the right. I even hit you. When I think what might have happened if you hadn't ignored me . . .' She choked back a sob. 'I'm so sorry.' She buried her face in her hands.

Rosie's good arm went out. 'Hey, don't be silly. Mum . . . hey.' She shook at the thick auburn hair.

Harry, who had watched silently, put his hand on hers, so they were both joined in her mother's hair. 'That goes for me, too,' he said. 'Right at the start I knew what they were like and then I believed them instead of you.'

Rosie leaned into her mother's hair and gripped Harry's

hand harder. 'Stop it, both of you. Everything's going to be all right now; I know it is.'

For many moments they were pressed together; then her mother sniffed the tears away and said, 'I nearly forgot. There's someone to see you.'

She untangled herself from them and crossed to the door. Peering out she said, 'She's awake. Come on in.' She opened the door wide and it was filled by Mr Jackson in his wheelchair, looking very stern, pushed by Jim Kitchen, the local newspaper editor.

They cleared a path so that Mr Jackson could get close to the bed. Rosie beamed at him. 'Oh, I'm so glad you're safe,' she cried out.

Mr Jackson's face was a tragic mask. He said gruffly, 'Rosie, you were right. I am a very silly old man, hm? You knew better than me all along, better than any of us, and I was bossy and foolish. All of us; all those old people, and me in particular, we owe you our lives.'

He was growing redder with each word and below his moustache 'his bottom lip began to quiver. Rosie could tell he was holding back tears. She picked up one long, veined old hand, kissed it and laughed. 'I do love you,' she said fondly.

A single tear squeezed from the corner of his eye and threaded its way down to the forest of his moustache.

Mr Jackson tipped his head down, unable to say more, desperately trying to hold back the tears. They all looked on in silence until Jim Kitchen broke the spell. 'Now, now. This isn't the time to be miserable. Rosie's a hero. The whole town's talking about her.' He looked at her mother. 'How about a picture for the paper?'

She looked proudly at her daughter. 'That's up to Rosie.'

The girl squirmed in her bed. 'Go on,' she wriggled, delighted, 'You don't want a picture of me.'

'Indeed we do, young lady,' said Mr Kitchen. 'You've saved ten people from certain death and ended years of misery for some of them. We certainly do.'

Rosie thought for a moment and said, 'Only if everyone else is in it, too.'

'Done!' said Jim Kitchen. He opened the door and beckoned to a young man with a camera who had been waiting outside. Everyone protested their reluctance, but Rosie insisted. The photographer took several pictures of them all sitting round the bed, until he was satisfied, then he left.

Mr Kitchen came over to her, serious. 'You are a remarkable young lady, Rosie Swallow. This town's not going to forget you.'

'Better get your camera ready again, Mr Kitchen,' she grinned. 'I'm going to win the race tomorrow, don't forget.'

No-one smiled back. There was silence round the bed. Rosie looked at each face in turn. 'What's the matter? Mum . . .?'

Her mother took her hand. 'Rosie, you've had very bad concussion. You knocked yourself out when you hit the deckchairs. You've been asleep a whole day. This is Saturday.' She looked at her watch. 'Darling, I'm sorry. The race starts in a few minutes.'

Rosie gasped. 'Then what are we doing? Come on; we'll be late.'

She threw back the covers and made to jump from the bed. 'Uh!' She would have keeled over and hit the floor if Harry had not been ready to catch her as she fell. A pain stabbed through her arm and scored angrily through the nerves in her back, burning at the base of her neck.

139

'You can't do it, Rosie,' said Harry. 'You dislocated your arm. We thought it was broken at first. It'll take a week or two at least before it's better.'

'But I can do it like this. I've got to be in the race. All this time . . .'

Mr Jackson cleared his throat, 'I'm afraid not, Rosie.' He unwrapped the bundle on his lap. Rosie had not noticed it before. It was his skates. He took out first one, then the other and turned it over. The axle was snapped; a wheel was missing.

'Must've happened when you hit the beach,' he said. 'They carted you off in such a hurry no-one noticed. We've been back scouring the pebbles for it, but no luck.

'I can probably make another one. It's been a long time, but I'm sure it will all come back to me. It will take weeks to get the right bits though, find a workshop and all that. Sorry, old girl, hm?'

Rosie lay back on the pillows and curled into herself. 'If you don't mind I'd like to go to sleep now,' she said.

Mr Jackson pushed himself closer. 'Rosie, if I could do anything . . .'

'It doesn't matter,' she smiled sadly. 'We're friends again; all of us. That's all I wanted.'

'Who knows,' said Jim Kitchen, affecting gaiety. 'Maybe there will be another chance.'

'Maybe,' said Rosie.

Mr Jackson reached out and stroked her head before Jim Kitchen pushed his wheelchair away. Harry leaned over and kissed her, followed by her mother. 'Will you be all right,' she whispered. Rosie nodded, a small, sad smile fixed to her face.

They all left, Rosie's mother closing the door quietly behind her. The room was still filled with the yellow light of the sun filtering through the curtains. There were faint

140

traffic noises from the town drifting in with the stain of sunlight. Behind them somewhere, thought Rosie, the skaters would be racing for the finish line.

She closed her eyes and bit her lip, and the tears came bubbling through. Her body lifted and fell as she was wracked with sobs. She wept until the light began to fade and she sank restlessly into sleep.

It was dark when she woke. A light from the corridor glowed in through a skylight above the door, and by it she could see the shadowed outline of a figure sitting in a chair beside her bed.

'Mum?'

'I'm here.'

'Who won, mum?'

Silence.

'Was it Bernard?'

Her mother sighed.

'It doesn't matter, Mum. Really. I don't mind anymore.'

'Yes; it was Bernard.'

'I guessed it would be. He was good. Tell him I said.'

'I will, darling. Try and get back to sleep.'

'Mum?'

'Yes, darling?'

'How fast?'

'One minute, five seconds.'

'Thanks. Goodnight mum.'

'Goodnight.'

Rosie was already asleep.

Fourteen

The next day was Sunday. Rosie had lots of visitors: Mr Kitchen, Mr Jackson; Mr Blamey (whose head bore the mark of the stone Rosie threw), came to thank her, saying not to worry about the stone. Already he seemed bigger and brighter in his wheelchair, now that he was out of the clutches of the Scribbinses.

Poor simple Millie came, and the policewoman, too.

And, of course, Harry and her mother. There was fruit and chocolates and flowers; but Rosie only lay on her pillows, smiling when urged to do so, but otherwise dispirited.

It was the same on Monday. Near the end of the day she had another visitor. She was alone, staring at the wall opposite her bed when a small knock sounded on the door. It pushed gently open and Bernard stood in the doorway, flushed and silent.

Rosie smiled, 'Congratulations.'

Bernard said: 'They told us at school today. About what you did.'

Rosie held up her bad arm, it was in a sling now. 'Done me arm in,' she grinned.

'They said you were nearly killed.'

Rosie shrugged, 'Nah!'

Bernard put down his school bag and fished into it. He pulled out an envelope and with it an ornament, a statue, that filled his fist.

'These belong to you, really,' he said. 'I got 'em in the race.'

The statue was a silver figure of a roller-skater in that straining moment of ultimate speed. It glinted in the light. Rosie's eyes widened. It was beautiful.

'The prize money's in the envelope,' said Bernard. 'You take 'em. Please.'

Rosie's mouth dropped open. 'You're giving them to me?'

Bernard nodded. 'You would have won if you'd been there. It didn't seem fair you should lose it after . . . after what you did.'

'Don't be daft,' said Rosie. 'I can't take them. Who's to say I would have won. Anything might have happened.'

Bernard held them out, but Rosie shook her head firmly. 'I'm glad it was you,' she smiled. 'It wouldn't have been the same if someone outside the town had won it.'

Bernard put the trophy and the envelope back in his bag and picked it up. 'I'll go then.'

He walked to the door, opened it and paused. He turned to look at Rosie once more and said; 'I'm sorry I cheated on you . . . you know, when we raced. It was only a sort of a joke.'

Rosie shook her head. 'That!' she said. 'I'd forgotten all about that.'

She paused. 'You could come again if you like; it gets dead boring in here.'

They grinned at each other. Bernard went out, closing the door behind him.

Two days later she was allowed home, and Bernard called on her there, too. She was ordered to remain off school until the following week; and she and Bernard played games together, but nothing changed her mood. Her old

143

spirit had gone and she played automatically, with no brightness in it.

On Friday as usual the local newspaper dropped on the doormat. Rosie picked it up. On the front page was her own picture, surrounded by Mr Jackson, Harry, her mother and Mr Kitchen, all sitting on the hospital bed.

Above the picture, in big, black type the headline read: ROSIE THE HERO!

Rosie the hero! The words sent a thrill through her and she flushed with pride. She read the story through; but then turned to the inside pages where there were details of the race and pictures of Bernard with the trophy. She tossed the paper aside as the desolation settled on her once more.

It was all over, she thought, and in a way the Scribbinses had won, after all.

There was a knock at the door. Her mother reached it first, and outside stood Harry behind Mr Jackson in his wheelchair. On his lap was a large cardboard box. They entered, grinning widely.

'Well, Rosie the hero,' said Harry. 'I've seen the paper.'

Rosie grinned back. 'Shut up,' she said softly.

Mr Jackson coughed, holding out the box. 'This is from everyone; from us here, the old people from the home, Mr Kitchen, the police, even Millie. For a conquering hero, what, hm?' He held out the box. 'Aren't you going to open it?'

She took the box and lifted the lid, pulling the contents into the light.

It was a pair of roller boots. Boots she had only dreamed of. Not the £30 kind she had yearned for and saved for; these were boots that could never have been hers in a hundred years. Boots that professionals used.

She had seen others like them with their price in three figures: more than £100!

The boots were stiff and shining and rich with the smell of leather. She held them in her hands and felt the power of them tingling her fingers: black leather trimmed with red, polished until it glinted like steel, and yet soft and streamlined. She stroked them, sighed lovingly over them. Beneath the boots the skates themselves gleamed brightly, a polished silver alloy edged with brilliant chrome. An idle flick of one black wheel sent it humming and humming.

Rosie rubbed the skates against her cheek. 'Oh, thank you,' she breathed. 'Thank you.'

Her mother and Harry hugged each other happily. Mr Jackson coughed loudly, stabbed a finger into the air triumphantly, and said, 'And now for the one-minute dream!'

Rosie looked at him and smiled. 'This is the most wonderful present I've ever had. Honestly. But I don't think I care about the one-minute dream any more.'

Mr Jackson was aghast. 'Not Care? Rosie, we've been so close. You can do it, I know you can do it.'

'But my arm . . .'

'Nearly better,' he said, sweeping aside the objection. 'We'll need about a week for practice; you have to get used to the new skates. And your arm will need exercising. You can start that today, hm? We'll get down to the Esplanade morning and evening for a week. You should be ready to have a go at it by, let's see . . . next Saturday.' He clapped his hands with delight.

Rosie threw up her arms helplessly, 'If you say so,' she laughed.

For the remainder of that week, and all the next he was waiting patiently at the flagpole. He urged her and

145

corrected her, and put her through spins and jumps and circles to improve her balance until he was happy that the new skates were as much a part of her as his had been.

In the evenings, too, he was waiting; and they raced when they could, him timing her. And at the end of every day she would skate wearily home to oil her skates and polish the gleaming leather before she slept.

'You're not overdoing it?' asked her mother.

'No; I love it,' said Rosie. She frowned. 'But I'm not sure I'll be ready for Saturday.'

She said so to Mr Jackson the next morning. He held up his hand. 'It has to be Saturday,' he said.

'But why can't we take another week, just to be sure,' asked Rosie.

'I have my reasons,' was all he would say. 'And anyway, you can do it.'

On Friday morning she cut the time down to one minute three seconds. Her body was wracked with the effort. Her arm and knee ached and her lungs pumped wildly to recover.

Mr Jackson was delighted, but Rosie wasn't so sure.

'I'll never be ready,' she gasped.

'Of course you will.' He gave her arm a squeeze.

'I need you to do it, for both of us,' he smiled.

She smiled, too, but she was worried.

She went back home for breakfast before she left for school. The weekly newspaper had been delivered. It lay on the mat. She picked it up and unfolded it. She was surprised, once again, to see her own picture dominating the front page. Beside the picture the giant headline read: GO FOR IT, ROSIE!

Below it the story explained how Rosie had been robbed of the chance to compete in the race, and to achieve her one-minute dream. It explained how she had

146

saved the old people from the fire, and as a special thank you from the town Rosie was to be given a chance to do what she had dreamed of.

At twelve noon on Saturday the Esplanade would be cleared to enable her to attempt to skate its length in under one minute. Anyone who wanted to go along and watch would be welcome.

As she read the story, Rosie went cold. Saturday. Tomorrow! Rosie looked up and saw her mother looking back at her from the far end of the hall. Rosie held out the newspaper. 'Did you know about this?'

Her mother nodded.

Rosie was dizzy with dismay. 'Tomorrow. That gives me twenty-four hours. That's all. I'm not ready.'

'Mr Jackson thinks you are.'

'He's in a wheelchair; I'm the one on the skates!'

'Mr Jackson thinks you can do it; and so do I.' Her mother walked forward. 'But if you don't want to we can put it off. No-one will mind, truly.'

She saw the muscles work in Rosie's jaw as her daughter clenched her teeth and the old familiar, stubborn gleam lit up her eyes.

'Hm!' was all she said, pushing past. 'I'd better get breakfast or I'll be late for school.'

Her mother smiled after her as she disappeared into the kitchen.

That evening, after school, Mr Jackson was waiting on the Esplanade with a copy of the paper on his lap. He could tell that she had already seen the story. 'Not cross, Rosie? Hm?' he asked.

She pretended a frown. 'So that's why Saturday was so important.'

He nodded. 'We set it up between us: Harry, Jim Kitchen and I.'

147

She grinned. 'I'm not cross; but I'm frightened. I still haven't done it yet. Why should it be any different tomorrow?'

'Just trust me Rosie. Tomorrow you will be under pressure, like you were with the fire and the Scribbinses. That will be what does it.'

'That was different. I was terrified. I've skated down the Esplanade for months. A few people watching won't make any difference.'

They practised hard. It was their last chance. Mr Jackson said she should spend Saturday morning taking things easy before the race.

'Eat a light breakfast early,' he said. 'Then relax. Watch television, read, anything. I don't want to see you down here until ten minutes before we start. We'll have a warm-up first, but that's all. Otherwise you'll be worn out before we begin.'

All evening she was quiet. Harry came for supper and he and her mother tried snatches of conversation, but Rosie only answered in single words, before she was absorbed again in her own thoughts. She sighed. 'I think I'll go to bed early.'

'Good idea,' said Harry. 'Can I give you a lift down to the Esplanade tomorrow?'

'Aren't you doing the deckchairs?'

'What? And risk getting them in your way?' he grinned. 'No, I decided to keep them clear. Going to cheer for you instead.'

'Thanks.' She kissed them both and climbed the stairs to bed.

The night passed slowly. It seemed that she lay turning and stretching for hours, while the past drifted in and out of her thoughts like dark fishes among deep reeds.

And then, suddenly, it was tomorrow. Her mother was

148

shaking her gently. 'Good morning, hero,' she smiled. 'Breakfast?'

Rosie pushed her breakfast cereal around the bowl for half an hour, hardly touching it. She checked her skates over carefully, and sighed and sat and checked them again. She fidgeted from one thing to another, the minutes dragging slowly by, until finally Harry arrived, and it was time to go.

The three of them climbed into his car and drove to the Esplanade. They passed increasing numbers of people, all walking towards the beach.

The pedestrians increased until there was a constant ribbon of them, all moving in the direction Harry was driving. Rosie began to fidget. They turned into the Esplanade and as Harry drove the length of the road towards the starting point Rosie's mouth dropped open in dumb amazement.

The sea could not be seen for the crowds. All along the Esplanade was a thick band of people standing, waiting. She heard a voice call, 'There she is, in the car!' And the crowd turned as one to see.

'Well done, Rosie,' came a shout.

'Hurray!' came another; and in no time the whole Esplanade was a sea of cheering, clapping faces all shouting for Rosie.

'Take me home,' she said, sinking terrified into the seat.

Her mother laughed, gently gripping her hand. 'You can do it, Rosie. I know you can. Don't give in now. It's so close. We're all with you.'

Rosie nodded, holding tight to her mother, and the crowds were oblivious to the paleness of her face. She stepped, shaking, from the car and the noise climbed to a crescendo. Jim Kitchen was waiting on the road by the flagpole. A breeze blew and a forest of multicoloured flags snapped and cracked above her. There was a platform beside the flagpole, covered in a vast Union Jack flag. A man was standing on it. He wore an extravagant purple robe with fur round the edges, and an old-fashioned, three-cornered hat.

Jim Kitchen stepped forward and took her hand. 'Hello, Rosie. Nervous?'

She nodded.

He leaned down close to her, pointed to the man in purple and said, 'That's the town mayor. He wants to meet you. You game?'

She nodded again, her knees all but buckling as she did so. Jim Kitchen led her by the hand up the platform steps. She was shaking all over. Suddenly a loudspeaker blared out. It had been lashed to the flagpole, close to her ear, and it echoed in others that had been placed down the length of the Esplanade, 'Pray silence for his Worshipful, the Mayor . . .'

It went on, but Rosie didn't hear. The Mayor was pumping her hand, beaming at her. His voice and his face seemed far away to Rosie, who was swallowed up by the noise and the sea of faces looking up at her on the raised platform.

The Mayor had a kind face. He put an arm round Rosie and led her across to a microphone.

'They want you to say something,' he whispered. She shrank back further. 'I haven't done anything yet,' she croaked, and heard her own terrified voice echo down the line of loud speakers, 'anything yet . . . anything yet . . . anything yet.'

The crowd was delighted. They clapped and cheered, while Jim Kitchen led Rosie down to where Mr Jackson, beside the flagpole, was smiling up. The loudspeakers were blaring again.

Mr Jackson waved it all carelessly away. 'Take no notice. They are just saying what's going to happen next. Better get your skates on, and I'll explain.'

Rosie sat down and pulled on her boots as Mr Jackson spoke. 'They are using a proper starting gun, and an electronic timing device, so it will be absolutely accurate. I want you to warm up as usual. Take your time. Don't let them hurry you. Harry is going to drive me up to the other end. I want to be there when you finish. They've got a big clock up there showing the seconds so we'll know straight away how you did. And there's lots of foam rubber against the railings, so you don't have to worry about slamming into them or slowing down. Just keep going at maximum speed.'

He pulled her down and kissed her on the cheek. 'Good luck, Rosie,' he said. He made to say something else, stumbled over the words, and muttered again, 'Good luck.' He turned away.

'Don't leave me here,' she said. 'I need you.'

She turned to her mother. 'Mum; all these people . . .' she pleaded. She lifted her arms in a gesture of helplessness and let them drop.

'They're on your side, Rosie. They're cheering for you.' She kissed her daughter.

Rosie peered down the Esplanade. On each side a wall of people waited, the noise gradually subsiding to a buzz of expectation. There were people at windows and on balconies in the houses overlooking the Esplanade, and people on the beach who would see nothing but who could fit nowhere else, and who would have to be content with hearing.

A quietness had settled. All eyes were on Rosie.

Jim Kitchen walked up once more. With him was a man with a small pistol. 'This is the starter, Rosie,' said Jim Kitchen. 'He's got a gun and it makes a good noise, so you'll hear it all right.

'Good luck' he grinned. 'I know you can do it.'

He left quickly before Rosie could open her mouth to speak.

'When you're ready, Rosie,' said the man with the gun. 'Take your time.'

The crowd was hushed, watching. 'Good luck, Rosie,' a small voice piped thinly through the crowd. She looked up and saw Bernard and a group of school friends waving furiously.

She waved back. Somehow she felt better for seeing faces she recognized. She nodded to the man with the gun. 'I'm ready,' she said.

A line had been painted on the ground, running out from the flagpole across the path. She stood poised with one skate touching it, took some deep breaths, and nodded again.

Nothing moved, and there was no sound but the flags cracking. Ahead was a narrow corridor of black asphalt hedged with a forest of bodies, every face turned towards her, waiting eagerly.

'Marks,' called the starter. A flag cracked; someone dropped something; far off a baby wailed and a voice said, 'Shhh.'

'Set.' Crack, crack went the flags.

A silence solid as stone covered everything. And yet it hung fragile as a shattered nerve.

The next instant the crack of the gun rent the air; above it and around it, following after, came the swelling roar of the crowd.

Rosie's limbs went into reflex action. They leapt like a

convulsion. She hardly knew what was happening. Her limbs moved despite her. The sharp, stinging bark of the gun hung in the air, and the crowd was a furnace roar.

To the spectators she appeared as a speeding blur, but Rosie knew better. The co-ordination was not perfect; she was flinging herself wildly. Where was the rhythm? The rhythm she had found on the day of the fire?

The fire. It came back to her. The boom of the exploding can and the instant roar of the flames. She could feel the heat from them and heard the car engine revving wildly behind her, and she knew she must beat down the panic if she was to survive.

The rhythm returned. Gradually the concentration took hold, panic diminished, and the roar of the flames and the engine's wild growl became the cheers of the crowd, hurling her onwards, urging her wildly. And the rhythm grew and the strength grew and she allowed herself one thought, just one – 'They're cheering for me!' – before she drove the distraction from her mind and found more power, more push in her driving stride.

The boots sang over the ground as brief snatches of voices rushed up and clipped off before they were finished; and through it all the crowds leapt and screamed their encouragement: 'Look at her go!'

'Keep back – '

'. . . pretty, too.'

'She'll do it!'

'Yes,' thought Rosie. 'I will do it. I will do it!' And with every nerve in her body she knew this was her moment.

A sixth sense took over, and as the wild blur of faces went flashing by Rosie was no longer among them. A strange feeling absorbed her; a sense of being above the crowd, watching her own body below on a thin ribbon of

153

asphalt, billowing on at a blinding speed towards the finish.

The crowd was in a frenzy. She caught the boom of a loudspeaker as she passed, conveying her progress to those who could not see, '. . . forty-two, three; I think she's going to make it.'

Behind her the crowd closed in, the narrow asphalt corridor vanishing as they surged up on her arrowing figure.

'Forty nine, fifty . . .'

Rosie wanted to sing out as her spirit snatched more speed. She sucked up the asphalt and spat it out behind her. And ahead the giant clock with its solitary hand tapped out the seconds inscrutably: fifty-five, fifty-six . . .

The world was a red blur at the corners of her vision; the noises rose and mixed to a wild crimson shriek of indistinguishable sounds; and the foam rubber on the railings filled her eyes as it rushed closer.

With a wild yell of exhilaration she threw open her arms and the crowd's scream reached a new, shattering crescendo as she cannoned into the thick, pillowing foam. The storm of noise vanished in a fog as she hung, momentarily buried there; then she was shot backwards by the foam rubber into the path.

Something caught her. The noise was a fury that hurt her ears, but still she laughed, looking up to see Harry who was laughing, too, his arms firmly wrapped round her shoulders.

Then she was up and out of his grasp, looking round, seeking and finding Mr Jackson in his chair beside her mother. She flung herself cannoning into the chair, hugging him close to her; laughing, perhaps crying, she didn't know. The power of her affection shoved the wheelchair backwards and only the pressing throng saved them from skimming together into the road.

Mr Jackson's eyes were bright with happy tears and he chortled, sang out, 'Look at the clock; look at the clock!'

Harry lifted her clear, to where she could see it over the heads of the cheering crowd. It was stopped just short of one revolution, the black hand nearly vertical: fifty seven. Fifty seven seconds!

And as they drank it in the loudspeaker confirmed it for those who could not see, and the roar of approval along the Esplanade became a physical barrage that swept back Rosie's hair as she laughed.

She reached out her hand to her mother and to Mr Jackson, but the crowd was too quick. She was swept up, lifted high over their heads to a perch on Harry's shoulder.

'Mr Jackson,' she cried. 'Get Mr Jackson.' And the word rippled out through the crowd until he, too, appeared over their heads, high and nervous but firmly held, with Rosie's mother close by.

And surrounded by the delighted crowd, lifted high and laughing bright tears, they were carried back down the asphalt Esplanade to the official congratulations of the Mayor in his ceremonial robe, and to the flags that crackled in the breeze.

Run With the Hare

LINDA NEWBERY

A sensitive and authentic novel exploring the workings of an
animal rights group, through the eyes of Elaine, a sixth-
form pupil. Elaine becomes involved with the group
through her more forceful friend Kate, and soon becomes
involved with Mark, an Adult Education student and one of
the more sophisticated members of the group. Elaine finds
herself painting slogans and sabotaging a fox hunt. Then
she and her friends uncover a dog fighting ring – and things
turn very nasty.

£1.95 ☐

Hairline Cracks

JOHN ROBERT TAYLOR

A gritty, tense and fast-paced story of kidnapping, fraud
and cover ups. Sam Lydney's mother knows too much.
She's realized that a public inquiry into the safety of
a nuclear power station has been rigged. Now she's
disappeared and Sam's sure she has been kidnapped, he can
trust no one except his resourceful friend Mo, and together
they are determined to uncover the crooks' operation and,
more importantly, find Sam's mother.

£1.95 ☐

ARMADA

SCRAMBLED
L · E · G · S

JAHNNA N. MALCOLM

Rocky: hot tempered
Mary Bubnik: worst dancer ever
Gwen: shortsighted and sharp-tongued
McGee: ice-hockey fanatic
Zan: head permanently in the clouds

Five friends at Deerfield's Academy of Dancing. What do they have in common?
THEY ALL HATE BALLET.

Follow the hilarious exploits of the gang, and their continual battle against the Bunheads, in this exciting series of 6 books:

1.	"We Hate Ballet!"	£2.25	☐
2.	The Battle of the Bunheads	£2.25	☐
3.	Stupid Cupids	£2.25	☐
4.	Who Framed Mary Bubnik?	£2.25	☐
5.	The Lucky Stone	£2.25	☐
6.	"Save D.A.D."	£2.25	☐

ARMADA

Barmy Jeffers
J. H. BRENNAN

Barmy Jeffers and the Quasimodo Walk	£1.95	☐
Return of Barmy Jeffers and the Quadimodo Walk	£1.95	☐
Barmy Jeffers and the Shrinking Potion	£2.25	☐

When schoolboy Barmy Jeffers stumbles through a Möbius Warp into a crazy fantasy world, his main concern is how to get home. He enlists the help of Ben, a dwarf, Bong, a mad cleric, Facecrusher, an awesome fighter, and many other colourful characters. His adventures bring him into contact with many gruesome and devilish creatures, before he finds the one man who can help him return home.

Fast moving and highly amusing adventures.

The
Counter Force
Series

GEORGE ERSKINE & IAN CAMERON

1	Beware the Tektrons	£1.95	☐
2	Find the Tektrons	£1.95	☐

The Counter Force comprises the four Melville children and their friends whom they invited to join forces against an alien force of intelligent electronic cells which live in computers and whose aim is to dominate the world.

ARMADA

The Pit

ANN CHEETHAM

The summer has hardly begun when Oliver Wright is plunged into a terrifying darkness. Gripped by fear when workman Ted Hoskins is reduced to a quivering child at a demolition site, Oliver believes something of immense power has been disturbed. But what?

Caught between two worlds – the confused present and the tragic past – Oliver is forced to let events take over.

£1.95 ☐

Nightmare Park

LINDA HOY

A highly original and atmospheric thriller set around a huge modern theme park, a theme park where teenagers suddenly start to disappear . . .

£1.95 ☐

ARMADA

All these books are available at your local bookshop or newsagent, or can be ordered from the publisher. To order direct from the publishers just tick the title you want and fill in the form below:

Name _____

Address _____

_____

Send to: Collins Childrens Cash Sales
          PO Box 11
          Falmouth
          Cornwall
          TR10 9EN

Please enclose a cheque or postal order or debit my Visa/ Access –

   Credit card no:

   Expiry date:

   Signature:

– to the value of the cover price plus:

UK: 60p for the first book, 25p for the second book, plus 15p per copy for each additional book ordered to a maximum charge of £1.90.

BFPO: 60p for the first book, 25p for the second book plus 15p per copy for the next 7 books, thereafter 9p per book.

Overseas and Eire: £1.25 for the first book, 75p for the second book. Thereafter 28p per book.

Armada reserve the right to show new retail prices on covers which may differ from those previously advertised in the text or elswhere.

ARMADA